# M U R D E R

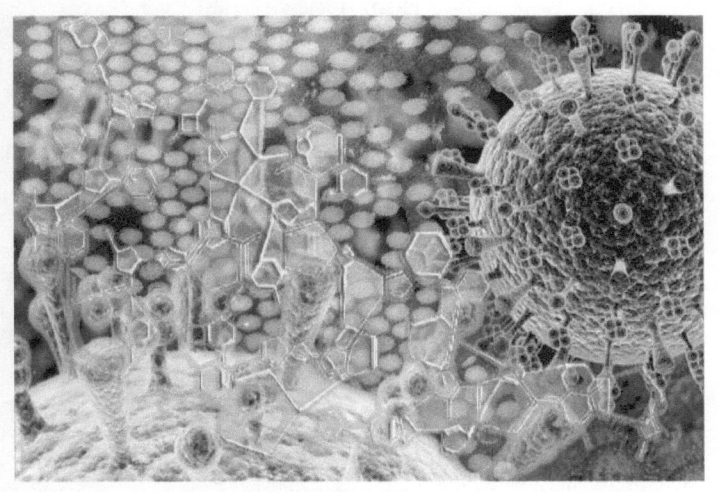

**DEREK E DYKES**

*Murder:* the crime of unlawfully killing a person, especially with malice aforethought. Derives partly from Middle English *murther,* from Old English *morthor;* partly from Middle English *murdre,* from Anglo-French, of Germanic origin; akin to Old English *morthor;* akin to Old High German *mord*; murder, Latin *mort-,mors* death, *mori* todie, *mortuus*: Dead, Greek *Brontos* - Mortal

Book One:
MADNESS

Book Two:
MAYHEM

Book Three:
MURDER

Special Thanks to Michelle, Branwyn, Micah, Nicole and Orey.
And to all my amazing friends and family
who never stopped believing in me and my children.

# prologue

Oppressive was not a strong enough word to describe the springtime heat in Mobile. Being located in lower Alabama, right on the Gulf of Mexico, the humidity only added additional levels of discomfort. Of course, my mother had loved growing up here; she was always cold, no matter how hot it was. I, on the other hand, had an unnaturally high body temp and like my grandfather, could never seem to get comfortable when the ambient temperature was over seventy-five. I found myself looking across the square and over the old buildings of Mobile's Historic District at the hazy silhouette of New Mobile, almost wishing that my next case was in the Dark Zone that existed in its shadow, just so I could cool off.

The three tiered fountain in Bienville Square offered its cooling mist to me as I entered the center of the park. Despite the already high humidity, the water coming off the fountain always seemed cool, and made it tolerable to be outside. I could see my team, along with several policemen, surrounding one of the decades-old wrought iron benches that circled the fountain, each one backing up to a flower bed and bushes of various types. When I got close enough, I could see bare feet sticking out of the foliage.

Zimmerman stood, staring at the body, hands in his pockets and a blank look in his eyes. Zim had a tough time dealing with the dead, especially after a few years ago, when his fiancée had been violently killed in the Dark Zone under St. Louis. He was holding his own, and doing a lot better, but Zim still had his moments when he retreated into the safety of his mind. I knew he'd be there when I needed him. More importantly, I'd be there when he needed me.

Michaels was tapping away at the control unit for a MR-CSA (Mobile Robotic Crime Scene Analyzer) that he'd brought to the scene. He looked up long enough to acknowledge me, and turned immediately back to monitoring the MR-CSA as it continued its E-MRI scan of the body.

"What do we have today, boys?" I asked sleepily. The coffee had not yet hit my brain and it had been a very long week.

"Well Ellie, this is what we in the forensics lab of the FBI refer to as a corpse. Although from the identification in the victim's wallet, we could call him Mr. Preston Woodridge".

I gave Michaels a look and reached out to take the ID. The holographic photo of Mr. Woodridge matched the face of the man lying on the ground. His right cheek was pressed into the dirt and there were bloodless scratches on his visible left cheek, likely caused by the branched he'd fallen into.

"No blood in the facial abrasions; he was dumped here," I said, bringing out a small penlight to illuminate the victims remains. "His skin looks glossy, Aaron. Any idea what the substance is?"

Michaels checked the MR-CSA controls, and shuffled through the data on the small, handheld screen. "Nope - the scan is finishing up now, but the data hasn't all been processed".

"Did he have any family, Ellie?" Zim asked quietly. He'd been like this all week; even though he had made great strides since the incident, this was a back step. I stood up and took my own handheld out of my pocket, and accessed the main database using his National ID number.

"Looks like he has a sister here in Mobile, and a brother in Queens," I answered, feeling a knot suddenly grow in my stomach. I hated having to give people news like this.

My attention turned back to the crime scene as I continued to examine the body. His clothes were almost new; the pants still had threads on the back pocket where the paper label had been attached. A mass of black curly hair covered his head, but he was well groomed and clean cut from all I could see. I gloved my hand and reached out to gently lift the victims arm, but found it was completely immobile.

"Wow. Rigor has already set in". I turned my attention to one of the policemen keeping people away from the scene. "Who's in charge of your unit, Officer?"

The young officer pointed to an older man who was standing maybe fifteen feet away. I whistled to get his attention, then smiled and motioned for him to come toward me.

"When was the last patrol before the body was discovered?" I asked.

"Three AM. We send out regular patrols every three hours since the zone opens up into the historic district only two blocks away".

"So the body was discovered at six, then?" I asked, mapping a timeline in my head.

"Yes Ma'am. Officer McDonald was coming through to do his rounds as a litter crew was doing their weekly on the foliage. They converged on this area just as Officer McDonald did, and he called it in immediately".

Our conversation was cut short when the MR-CSA scanning the scene sounded a warning siren. Red lights started flashing on its dome, continuing to do so even after Michaels cut the siren so we could all hear.

"Hazard Warning, Ellie!" Michaels called. "The E-MRI has picked up an unknown biohazard. Whatever it is, it's been tagged as lethal".

The squad of police officers each took several steps back, leaving me and my boys close up and personal with the apparently tainted corpse. "Damn it!" I shouted, reaching into one of the built-in drawers on the MR-CSA and pulling out a large glass vial with a cutting tool built into the top. I took the device and used it to envelop the deceased forefinger. With a sharp turn of the metal iris atop the lid, the finger was quickly and cleanly removed. It dropped into the built-in hazard container that sealed itself immediately.

"Got a sample; lock it down, Michaels" I said, quickly backing away with Zimmerman. Michaels backed away too, all the while tapping in new commands into the mobile analyzer. The MR-CSA extended one of its few appendages, which flipped over and opened, revealing a high-powered laser which it aimed at the body. Usually we used recovery drones to burn away the dead that tended to pile up in the Dark Zone, but MR-CSA's were equipped with hazard removal lasers as well, for situations just like this. The laser beam fired, but instead of beginning the process of destroying the almost ceramic-looking tissue, the beam reflected off the corpse as soon as it had burned through the clothes, and hit a nearby storefront, knocking bricks and mortar onto the ground below. Michaels hit a different control; the colour of the beam shifted from red to blue, and widened two-fold. The more powerful laser beam stopped bouncing away from the victims' skin, and within seconds all that remained of the remains was a large, black smudge on the ground.

Smoke wafted up from the place where Mr. Woodridge had lain only moments before, and the police officers all gathered close to look at the carnage. Zim and Michaels huddled closer to me as I held up the only remaining portion of the deceased. In the small jar, closed tight for safety, sat a whitish, almost porcelain-looking finger. When I shook the vial, the finger tinkled against the glass, sounding like a piece of pottery being shaken in a vial.

# 1
## ⚘Thinking⚘

It's always an odd feeling watching the air you breathe bubble up in front of your eyes and float away. Despite the weight of the air tanks on my back, or the pressure of the diving mask on my cheekbones, I always had to remind myself that I wasn't drowning; but no matter how much I knew I was safe, the primal fear was still there inside. It burned like a fire, stoked by the inner voices we all have. Though I was an accomplished diver, having logged over five hundred hours underwater since I was a teenager, I still had to fight back the lump in my throat each time I suited up. Even when I dove almost every day, one of the odd little daemons trapped inside my brain would keep whispering fearful thoughts into my ears as the water enveloped me, telling me that the air won't last, or the mechanism will fail at a critical moment, and I will end up as food for the predatory fish that roamed the southern coastal waters.

It's not like I was alone here. My grandfather was the first diving partner I had, having taken scuba classes with me during one of the long summer breaks when I was twelve. He had wanted to take part in the documenting of the underwater ruins created in 2027 by Hurricane Joaquin when it, coupled with explosions from uncontrolled fracking beneath the city, finally accomplished the task of destroying New Orleans, and he and my grandma Jerri wanted me to go with them. We had learned early on that you never dove without a partner or two, especially in a sunken, devastated city like New Orleans. I paused from my thoughts, looking ahead of me to see Michaels and Zimmerman's helmet lights flashing down the remains of Interstate 10, and used the knowledge of their presence to beat my inner daemon back into his cage. I wasn't alone, and no matter what happened, I knew my boys were always looking out for me, just as much as I always looked out for them.

"Ellie," Michaels said over the small radio built into my headpiece. "Watch your step over here. I am starting to see debris from the plane crash; it all looks pretty sharp".

"I'll keep my eyes open Aaron. Thanks," I responded, noting the location of each out of place metal shard as we walked across the old Pontchartrain Bridge. The scattered wreckage gleamed against the murky backdrop of the dark water surrounding us, making it easy to tell which pieces of trash were new, and which ones had been here for twenty years or more. A few more yards ahead, the bridge ended, and Zimmerman was standing beside the fuselage of the X-999 Aircoach that had carried 300 people to their deaths almost a week ago. The gargantuan aircraft was decidedly out of place under the surface of the lake, and its carcass rose above us like the ruined buildings my grandfather used to photograph; it was desolate and unwelcoming. The knowledge that we were the first team to reach the main wreckage made it all the more eerie.

Zim was tagging a perimeter as the boat above us started dropping supplies. Underwater searchlights drifted slowly to the bottom, expanding their legs for a soft landing, and large packs of recovery supplies also pierced the veil of rubbish that floated between us and our recon craft. Over the years since its demise, the garbage from old New Orleans had started floating to the surface, only to get trapped and tangled together, forming a deadly net that dozens of divers had perished in just over the last five years. While the equipment was heavy enough to punch its way through, people were far more likely to get hopelessly trapped in the waste, which is why we had to walk our way into town.

Michaels and I made our rounds to each of the spotlights, activating the systems and targeting their beam on the plane, bringing daylight to this place for the first time in many years. After all the lights were turned on, I went to the main supply box that had dropped for us, and took out the switching device for the compact air tanks I'd need to go inside the plane. Michaels and Zim silently adjusted the equipment on my back, and Zim gave me a nod when it was time to hold my breath. When they disconnected my main tank, I could feel the pressure change both in my mask, and in my chest as my inner daemon started laughing and pounding to be released. I counted in my head, seeing bubbles of fresh, life-giving air float up to rejoin the atmosphere above. When I reached twenty, I turned my head to Zim, and he held up one finger. Ten more seconds passed by, and I could feel myself getting light headed. Zim still stood, holding up a single digit, his eyes turning back and forth from me to the work Michaels was doing on my back.

Finally, Zim dropped his finger and I could feel the pressure adjust as oxygen flowed into my mask. As much as I wanted to gasp for air, I knew that wouldn't help, so I carefully let out the stale breath of air that had sat in my lungs for too long, and took a long, slow breath in.

"What happened, Zim?" I asked over the radio. "That didn't seem to go very well".

Before Zimmerman could offer an answer, Michaels stood up, saying "The connection flange they sent down had the wrong fitting. I had to improvise with parts from a different unit".

I nodded, cutting the transmission, and trying to give Michaels a reassuring smile through my diving mask. The less we spoke down here the better; doubly so for me since I was now on a limited, albeit much more compact, air supply. I had at most twenty minutes of air, and one hell of a lot of work to do in that time. Letting my boys take my main air tanks off my shoulders, I turned back to the fallen aircraft, and climbed onto the rough, jagged aluminum edge where the wing had once joined the fuselage. Once I was balanced and had kicked away any loose pieces of metal, I approached the hatch. Turning the handle on the outer door, I could feel the mechanism working effortlessly in my hands as the doorway unsealed and swung open, drifting aside and granting me access to the tomb that waited for me. The plane had crashed nose down, burying the pilot's control room well underneath the 'street level' we were on, but we were lucky that the hatches were all still above ground. At least we didn't have to dig to get to them, and we didn't have to cut through the body of the plane. I looked into the dark, slanted doorway before me, held a deep breath, and went inside the multi-level aircraft.

I had to raise the plane if its floatation device had survived the crash. With the X-999 supposedly being 'uncrashable', it had now become the Titanic of the airways, and for the last four days, all fifteen-hundred of them had been grounded worldwide. The economic repercussions were almost as bad as the cost in human life. With room for 300 plus passengers, and a crew of twenty, this was the worst air disaster involving a single craft since the Heathrow bombings six years ago. While that had involved multiple aircraft, all of them had been blown up on the runway, so none of them had crashed; they hadn't even gotten off the ground. Six X-999's were targeted in what looked like a terrorist attack. We found out later that a rival company was behind the explosions, trying to reduce public confidence in the 'uncrashable' X-999. As soon as I set foot inside the sunken aircraft, I knew this was totally different.

The plane sat at a near forty-five degree angle, so getting down to the cockpit would be one hell of a lot easier than getting back out. The water was murky, and thick enough with sludge and muck that even with my helmet's built-in superbrights, my visibility was a few feet at best. I passed the galley, and made note of the body of an attendant sitting strapped down in an emergency seat. Something about her didn't look right, but I scarcely had time to check her out with the small amount of oxygen I had, so I continued into the 'first class' section of the plane. It was decorated with fine, intricate designs in the carpet and ceiling, and had the plane not been filled with water, it could have almost felt like the lobby of a fine hotel. The seats swiveled so passengers could face each other and talk. Once again I noted several dozen corpses, each one appearing out of the darkness as I passed by. Considering my main job with the FBI was forensic criminology, I had seen more than my fair share of the deceased over the years. The only reason I was here was because my diving experience outpaced the local TSA team by at least 100 hours; that and at five foot two, I was small enough to navigate through the cabin of a sunken plane without getting trapped.

Approaching the nose of the plane, the walls of the cabin started to show signs of the outer damage, and I knew I was not only underwater, but underground as well. According to the specs Zim had pulled before we left Mobile, the X-999 had three emergency releases for the floatation system. One of the pulleys was in the rear of the plane. Since the rear section had broken away midair and crashed into what was once the lower ninth ward, that knowledge was of no use to me right now. It was because the rear separated from the main body that we had just now located the cabin of the plane; the primary signaling devices had been in the planes' tail, so three days were spent searching the old ninth ward for wreckage that simply wasn't there.

The primary floatation switch was in the cockpit, and by design was supposed to be pulled by the crew before hitting the water. Since that hadn't happened, we knew something had to be wrong with the crew before the crash, which was another reason my team was here.

The cramped, damaged corridor was getting to be a tight fit, even for my small framed body. I did manage to make my way to the cockpit, gingerly stepping past the floating body of another crew member. I gently brushed him aside, saying in my head *"we'll get you home - I promise"*. The door to the cockpit was open, and its contents held the worst damage I had seen so far. The front of the plane had collapsed on impact, crushing its occupants in an accordion-like mesh of flesh and computer equipment. Wherever the switch was in the cockpit, there was no chance of it being activated now.

"Zim" I asked quietly, opening the comm to my boys outside. "Cockpit switch is a no go. Where is the third?"

"Just outside the cockpit Ellie," Zim answered, sending the diagram over to my wrist-mounted display. I looked around, and saw the discrete lever behind the floating corpse I had conversed with moments before. As I made my way around the small secondary galley towards my goal, I gently moved the dead man aside and reached over to pull the lever, feeling the floatation system rumble to life underneath my feet.

"That's it boys," I said into the comm. "Ditch the equipment, and get back to your pickup spot. I'll see you both topside".

Michaels and Zimmerman acknowledged, heading off for the shore. Meanwhile, I could feel the pressure changing around me. I still had ten minutes of air left, and the estimate on raising the plane was a scant seven minutes, so I worked my way back around the body towards the entry hatch. It was now, that my primary goal had been reached, that I took a moment to look closely at the dead man floating around me. I saw the typical open, glazed over eyes that I would expect from a drowning victim who'd been submerged for days. His exposed flesh was untouched by fish, as none had entered the sealed, though leaky cabin of the plane. His skin shined in the light of my helmet superbrights, glittering with an almost porcelain-like sheen. I was immediately taken back to Bienville Square, and the case we'd been working on when we were called in to assist here in New Orleans. I gently reached out my gloved hand, and tapped on the backside of the corpse' hand. It felt like I was tapping on glass.

I knew when we broke the surface and the water started pouring out, his unfettered carcass would be tossed around like a rag doll, so I decided to grant this poor soul a little dignity and strap him to a seat if I could. I moved to place him in one of the jump seats as best as I could. Like the body we'd found in Bienville Square, this corpse was stiff and unyielding, so there was no way to adjusting his posture to accommodate seating him. Once I had him settled, I immediately went back to the first class section, and briefly checked each of the victims seated there as I passed through. I could hear the body of the plane move through the field of debris and trash above, each tendril of metal and garbage scraping against the plane as it rose from its watery repose. We were almost to the surface, so I kept pushing forward toward the hatch I had entered through. From what I could tell of the passengers and crew I passed on my way out, each one was locked into position, and had that same, odd porcelain-like quality to their exposed skin.

If I hadn't just seen this a few days prior back in Mobile, I'd swear there was something in the water. But I knew better, and there was no way I could believe that this was simply an accident.

********

## 2
### ❧Conflict❧

The cabin of the plane broke the surface and leveled out on the floatation system that I had triggered. This part of old New Orleans was under four-hundred fifty feet of water, and the ascent was slow enough that I didn't have to worry about any degree of compression sickness. When I stepped up to the door of the plane, I could see several boats circling, each one equipped with large lift arms for placing the wreckage on the barge that was slowly trudging through the water to retrieve the plane. A Coast Guard lifeboat pulled up close to the doorway, and I took the small jump into the craft and away from the now-floating graveyard behind me.

"They're all dead," I said to the lieutenant driving the small rescue boat.

"Really; Imagine that", he answered sarcastically. I rolled my eyes at him and slugged him on the upper arm.

"No, that's not what I mean. Of course they're all dead", I shot back, watching the man rub his now sore bicep. He looked at me with a glare as I continued. "They were likely all dead before they hit the water. And that, my friend, turns this from an accident site to a potential terrorist event".

By the time we all met on shore, the news of the murders had ripped its way through the recovery squad. I met Michaels and Zimmerman at the dock and filled them in on the grisly details as we walked to the command center the Transportation Safety Administration had set up for this mission. Before we even walked in, we could hear the argument we were about to be drawn into.

Opening the door, the words of my boss, Jim Forrest, greeted my ears. His face sat on an oversized wall screen, looking more than a little irritated. There was a group of six men, all with their backs to the doorway, and all trying to get a word in edgewise as Forrest watched them argue. After a moment, Jim cleared his throat grabbing the attention of the men in the room.

"Gentlemen" Forrest began, his baritone voice pulling their attention to him. "Let me get a few things straight before anyone says another word". The men in the room, some in rescue garb and some in suits, all nodded, their body language relaxing a bit. "Now, don't get me wrong. I have the utmost respect for what you and your division deals with every day. But with that being understood, this crash has been one screw up after another for you".

One of the suited men sat back up, raising his voice to the screen in protest, but Forrest just looked down at the man, using the oversize display to exert a bit of intimidation over the crowd, and making himself look bigger than life as he stared down the man in a blue suit. When it was quiet again, he continued. "First, you follow the black box signal instead of using the recon system, and waste three days recovering the hind end of the plane. A three hundred sixty-million dollar barge was also sunk when it ran into a submerged building left in the old ward. It will take at least a month to retrieve it, if it's even possible to get in a vessel large enough to raise it".

The men all looked to each other, some sheepishly turning their gaze down towards their feet.

"Then you discover that your best divers are too worn out from the goose chase they've been on, and are no longer safety compliant for a dive, so you happen to find out that one of my teams has diving experience, and you pull us away from our jobs to help".

"If you minded that much Jim," the blue suited man said, "you shouldn't have allowed them to come".

Forrest' scowl grew deeper as he responded, "Of course we don't mind helping. For God's sakes, Tuttle, over 300 people are dead after that crash! Of course we are going to help. What I object to is the treatment Agent Dyett is getting because she found out something that potentially throws the whole investigation out of your prevue".

Zim cocked a quizzical eyebrow as he turned to look at me, but all I could do was shrug my shoulders and listen as the man named Tuttle spoke again.

"Look Jim, I know she's exceptional, and I know all about her team and their accomplishments. But to say that everyone on that plane was murdered before it hit the water - well, it's absurd! How is someone going to go thru a planeload of almost three-hundred passengers and twenty crewmembers, systematically killing people in their seats, and then crash the plane into the water with no signs of any escape?"

Before Forrest could answer, I spoke up. "You are making assumptions Tuttle and putting words in my mouth".

The men turned to see me and my boys standing behind them. Tuttle turned back to Forrest on the monitor and asked "Did you know she was standing there?" Jim simply nodded an affirmative, then sat back to watch the fireworks.

Tuttle straightened himself up and walked up to me. "Now we do appreciate all your help Ellyandra..."

"Agent Dyett will do, thank you Mr. Tuttle. Now before you try and make your case, let me make something perfectly clear".

Michaels and Zimmerman both took a slow step back, leaving me face to face with the bureaucrat in the blue suit. "I have been an FBI criminologist for over six years now. In that time, I have personally examined and diagnosed thousands of different types of wounds, mutilations, attacks and desiccations both natural and man-made. Now oddly, I agree with you that the circumstances are absurd at the very least. But each of the people I saw in that plane were exposed to something, either accidentally or with cause, that led to their deaths before the plane went down - it's as simple as that. So unless you are suggesting that *I* somehow altered the bodies, or kept the flight crew from activating the floatation devices before impact, or God forbid, if you have no concern for your own people's exposure to something lethal, then I'd back off and let me and my boys do our jobs".

The men behind Tuttle hadn't approached him, leaving him physically vulnerable and more easily intimidated by someone (anyone) with any degree of self-confidence. As Tuttle stammered in front of me, trying to pull out words, Forrest jumped back into the fray with a suggestion. "Look, Tuttle. Your team should take the plane and find out why it crashed; let's make sure there we know exactly what happened from a transportation standpoint. However, as a crime scene, my team gets first crack at it. We'll share anything we find with you, you do the same for us, and we can all be one big, happy Governmental Agency again".

"Aren't we in different agencies Ellie?" Zimmerman asked, getting a quick 'hush' from me as a response.

********

# 3
## ◈Images◈

I had hardly seen my home or my girls for over a week. With the travelling to the outskirts of New Orleans, the recovery operation, and all the work that had come since, I had been working late, coming in early, and had even slept in my office more than I cared to think about. We had to set up a makeshift morgue in an unfinished sublevel of the Federal Building just to handle the large number of deceased. I'd been acting as an autopsy tech, forensic pathologist, and even a funeral director for almost seven days straight, and despite my high metabolism and upbeat worldview, I was weary to the bone.

My girls had already gone to sleep by the time I made it home. Granddaddy had been living with us since Christmas, so watching the girls in the evenings while I was holed up in the office was no trouble. Now that we'd gotten the basic grunt work out of the way, the rest of the investigation would be easier. At least, I kept telling myself that as I went into the kitchen, poured a glass of Merlot, and asked the house computer to start my bath.

I didn't bother to turn on the lights this late at night. I couldn't take the chance of waking one of my sleeping darlings, since I was way too tired to give them the energy they deserved. Of course my decision to meander through the dark would haunt me as my bare feet somehow found every lost building block, action figure and craft item they'd missed in their evening cleanup. I don't get angry about a few missed toys; Hell, the girls just turned five, not fifteen. Kids miss things like toys or other things that need cleaning up. What they don't miss, I'd learned in my first few months as a parent, was generally anything that you didn't want them to hear.

When I hit the top of the stairs, I went to the nearest wall control unit and hit the button for a silent sweep from the minibot that vacuumed my home. That would at least clear the floor space for more action-packed adventures the next day, and it would keep me from injuring myself more than I already had. As I closed the cover panel to the control unit, something about the time of night, lack of sleep, and oddly moving shadows brought my eyes to the door of the room where my grandfather was sleeping. It used to be my room, until the night a crazed friend, sick out of his mind, snuck into my home and tried to kill me. I'd never been more frightened before that moment, and only a few moments since had even come close. I'd had all the bedrooms renovated, but the oak bedroom door Roberts had plowed through was an antique, and had been repaired instead of replaced. Tonight, as it had many nights since, that door guarded my dear grandfather as he snored away peacefully. Also tonight, as it had done many times, flickers of light caught its carved beauty, casting miniscule shadows in the doors' artwork. Despite the hand-worked relief, all I could see were the parts that had once been splintered off, and I could almost hear my own screams.

I shuddered, and moved into my bedroom, setting the wine glass on the edge of my nightstand, and casually tossing clothes here and there to finally de-stress from the day. It was nights like this that I was truly grateful for a home that cleaned itself. I gazed at the garden tub through the half opened door that separated my bathroom from my bedroom, and decided that if I took anything longer than a quick dip, I'd probably fall asleep in the water. I cleaned up as fast as I could before drying off and hitting the sack, almost asleep before my head hit the pillow, and leaving a perfectly good glass of wine nearly untouched.

********

The next day started off with good news. The last of the plane wreckage had finally been hauled up, and the MR-CSA's had finished their scans of the debris. By this time tomorrow, we'd be able to suit up and head to the holorecreator. The even better news was a box full of evidence that Tuttle and his men had deemed would likely be of interest to our investigation. The box was sitting on the shift chief's desk waiting for my signature when I got to work.

After stopping by to pick up the care package Tuttle had sent us from the crash review site, I bypassed my office and took the lift down to the unfinished levels we were using to handle all of the dead. Three hundred-four men, women and children, (not counting the pilot, co-pilot and cabin crew) had been laid out in various positions on gurneys and floor-pads in our makeshift morgue, and the temp on the entire level had been turned to 28 degrees, to preserve these poor folks until they could be processed and claimed by their next of kin. That meant that we had to work dressed like Eskimos, but the plus side of it was, at least we weren't sweating to death. That, and there was free coffee- lots of free coffee. Over the week, we'd been able to process almost two hundred, and sent them along to their families. That kind of work is tough on the soul, and demands equal parts respect for the dead and lighthearted banter, to keep the gloom and morbidity from taking permanent hold.

"Look what Santa sent us, kids!" I cried, entering the open workspace and walking right past the parka that had been set aside for me. "Tuttle and his men did their part. We've got a full E-MRI being processed for the holorecreator, and a box full of good old fashioned evidence that his men thought we would want 'hands-on' time with".

Michaels looked up from the central table where we'd all been working over the last week. I walked over and placed the sealed box on the workspace next to him, and he and Zim both gathered round to see what we'd been sent.

The packing slip read like a laundry list from a garbage collector. Most of the items were small and innocuous; a metal tin with an unidentified powder (that had turned to mush in the waters of the lake), pieces of computer equipment that had not been identified as part of the plane, or logged as passenger carry-ons, what looked to be a metal vial – sans lid or cap – that had been bagged as having a low level radiation signature, and more pieces and parts of loose scraps of garbage that likely meant less than nothing in the grand scheme of an investigation.

I was just about to completely lose any thanks I had for Tuttle when I saw, at the bottom of the box, a prosthetic leg, wrapped in an evidence bag.

"Michaels, didn't we have one body that was missing a leg?" I asked, holding the metal and plastic appendage aloft.

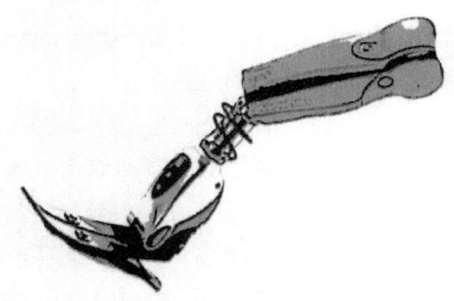

Aaron started walking thru the hundred-or-so 'guest' as he had come to call them, and quickly found the man I had been thinking of.

"Yup: Passenger 303. He's been scanned and cleared for anything dangerous, but we haven't processed him yet. Initial scan found no identification and only a few personal items in his possession.

"OK, Michaels. 303, right?" I muttered, taking the prosthetic over to a SR-FDA (Stationary Robotic Forensic Data Analyzer) and scanning it into the database. "Can you pipe him up to the holo-morgue?"

"He's right here, El. Why just go the old fashioned way?"

"Point taken, but what happened to the last of these folks we tried to examine down here?" Aaron lowered his head a bit, placing the sheet back over Passenger 303.

"Parts broke off" he answered quietly.

"Yep. These folks don't have rigor; whatever killed them has pretty much turned them into a porous stone, lightweight and brittle. So if I'm going to try and do a prosthetic fitting…"

"You'd rather not have the legs breaking off into unworkable shards. Sorry Ellie – I wasn't thinking".

"I got him, Ellie" Zim said, jumping in and starting the process of building the holographic body in one of the holo-morgues upstairs. So much of this situation had been low tech; I knew Zim was feeling useless, so anything he wanted to contribute was fine with me. The SR-FDA beeped its affirmative that the scan was complete, so I placed the leg back in its box, grabbed a coffee, and headed upstairs to see what the computers had reconstructed for me.

********

I loved the technology in the holorecreator; the ability to place yourself into a simulation and feel, smell and handle the environment around you was invaluable as an investigator. Only downside was the full-body Ferrin suits one had to wear in order to make the magic work. They were skin tight, hot as Hell, and far too easy to damage. The Holo-morgue, on the other hand, was never meant to be a full immersive simulator. It had one purpose – build the scanned body down to the last detail – and this, coupled with Ferrin gloves and a voice interface that acted on every command, made the holo-morgue one of the best tools in my toolbox.

Opening the door to the holo morgue had become one of our ways of surprising each other with something light hearted, to help keep the edge off. I never knew if Zim had programmed the deceased in question to be dancing, doing jumping jacks, or just standing, waiting for me to begin. We'd promised ourselves that we'd never do anything that could be considered disrespectful; that's not what this was about. Each of the individuals we'd processed since the crash had been dehumanized in their death – turned into objects instead of people. Giving their holographic images some degree of life was more of a way to bring back their humanity than anything else. Still, even knowing where we were coming from, it was almost too much on my nerves to walk in and see passenger 303 standing on one leg, balanced against the air, and handing his prosthesis to me.

I took the Ferrin gloves from the small table just inside the door, then 'grabbed' the photonic limb and strapped in gently into place. It took some degree of training to use any of the holo equipment, but if I'd ever doubted my dexterity with these units in the past, the last week of overuse had convinced me otherwise. It felt as natural as tying my shoes, working with the unfamiliar equipment, and within two minutes I had Passenger 303 standing on his own two legs again.

"Please take off your coat, 303," I asked aloud, then added, "and empty your pockets as well".

The holographic corpse complied, moving slowly through his coat pockets and placing various trinkets on the exam table. He then removed his coat and hung it midair on a non-existent holographic hook.

Now the odd part began, as I tossed his coat away into the nothingness it had come from, and used the Ferrin gloves to open his chest to look around. The computer kept beeping in error as I tried to manipulate the 'petrified flesh' of the man. We'd run into that problem early on, but Zim had programmed the unit to treat all minerals in the simulation as though they were flesh. It made working with bones an 'interesting' process, but overall we'd been able to adapt. Something about this one was different.

"Computer, get Zimmerman down here," I commanded, taking my hands out of the uncooperative holo-flesh and redirecting my examination to the prosthetic leg. While I waited for Zimmerman to come troubleshoot the code, I might as well look at what I could examine properly. The leg was fairly compact, but it attached easily, not only via straps and such, but also to electrodes implanted in the skin of the deceased. A small computer unit just below the leg stump had been designed to move the lower portion accordingly, but all the hydraulics, switches and components I'd expect to see on a unit like this were missing. In place of the hydraulic cylinder that did the calf muscles' job was a heavy-looking compartment, with a slide and lock cover, almost like the bolt action on an old fashioned rifle.

When Zim opened the door, the hologram in front of me shimmered in the moving air. Zim closed the door behind him and settled in at the wall terminal, clicking and clacking away faster than any normal person should.

"That's weird Ellie; my last protocols for this condition are still in place, so something has to be different about this body. I'll need to reprocess the imaging at a cellular level to find out what. Can he wait until tomorrow?"

I almost missed what Zim had said, I was so engrossed by the odd prosthesis. "Um, yea. Sure. I can always go back downstairs and examine the real leg".

As we were on our way out, I stopped to take notice of the things Passenger 303 had removed from his pockets. His airline ticket could come in handy, I thought to myself. There was a metal lined piece that looked like a bottle stopper – seemed to match the metal vial in the basket of goodies that Tuttle had sent along. Most of the pocket contents were receipts and some other general garbage. But what caught my eye was the small cross the victim had held in his pocket. It was about three inches long, gold in colour and rather thin, almost like a crucifix. But the Christ figure on this ornament was unlike anything I'd ever seen before; the Christ was nailed upside-down to the cross, with His hands where the feet should be, and his legs spread far so the feet could be nailed where each hand would be. He wasn't upside down, so to speak, as His loincloth lay flat and tidy.

"What in the world?" Zim asked, looking over my shoulder at the twisted figure on the cross.

"I've never seen anything quite like it Zim. But I know a few people who may be able to help.

\*\*\*\*\*\*\*\*

I had a few people in mind to look over the cross; the kind of scholars who'd jump up and down, going 'ohhh' and 'ahhh' over something this unique. But first I'd have to find the real artifact in the physical belongings of Passenger 303. A quick drop back down into the unfinished levels, and the lift doors opened. Michaels was standing there, holding out the parka I'd procured for the work in this freezer.

"A week of this – you'd think we'd be used to it by now", Michaels commented, tugging his zipper up just a bit tighter under his chin.

"As my mother would tell you, we're not penguins, Aaron". I zipped up loosely and headed for the coffee pot. "Of course, she's say that if it was fifty degrees, let alone below freezing".

We walked back over to the workstation Michaels had set up, setting down our coffee cups and began to rifle through the 'evidence' Tuttle's people had sent. I took the prosthetic leg back out of the evidence bag, and took a closer look at the weird hollow chamber that replaced the internal mechanism. It looked as though it was custom built to hold something –but what I just couldn't put my finger on.

Setting the leg down, I walked down the rows of the deceased until I reached Passenger 303; there was a small lockbox of belongings underneath the gurney, which I tucked under my arm and took back to the workstation. I could've gone thru the meager contents right by the body, but working with others not only kept me warmer, but made me feel less conscious about literally being surrounded by the dead. That though in and of itself was *just creepy* enough to put the smallest extra spring in my step.

I set the lockbox on the table and lifted the lid. Sure enough, the contents matched what we'd seen in the holo morgue. I grabbed the airline ticket, hoping we'd get a partial name from the water-washed paper, but the ink had been ruined by Lake Pontchartrain. I took out the bottle-stopper, and looked it over. It was a gleaming brushed aluminum, with a synthetic cork applied to its length; rounded, cylindrical, and maybe an inch from top to bottom. I set it down on the workspace and went looking for the crucifix in the mess of candy wrappers, when Zim walked up.

"OK Boss, what can I do to help?" he asked innocently. "I've got the holorecreator building the whole plane, and we'll even have options for the passengers. What's next?"

I was still clawing through the lockbox of Passenger 303; my fingers just brushed up against something cold and metallic, and I only half-answered Zim. "Empty out that box Tuttle sent; I think I saw a match to this," I said, pulling out the metal stopper and placing it down on the table. Of course, Zim, being a literalist (like most computer programmers are) picked up Tuttle's box and dumped it all out on the workspace, spilling its contents out willy-nilly, and knocking my lockbox to the floor.

Michaels jumped back with a startled, "Damn it Zimmerman!" But before Zim could respond, and before I could say a word, we all stopped. The bottle-stopper started moving, gently rolling on its side across the odd path through the junk toward the vial that had been in Tuttle's evidence box. When they clanked together, you could see it was an obvious set; both were made of brushed aluminum, and the stopper looked to be a perfect fit to the vial.

"We'll I'll be damned," Zim said quietly.

"Not today, buddy," Michaels answered. "Not today".

********

I sat with a jeweler's loop, inspecting every crease and crevasse in the almost unholy-looking cross, while Zim and Michaels ran dozens of test on the metal vial and stopper. It was enough that I was cold (and out of coffee), but the series of exclamations and surprises one or the other kept uttering was almost too disturbing. I had just noticed some interesting markings near the loin cloth on the figure when I heard the SR-FDA calmly announce, "RADIATION WARNING".

"Radiation? Computer – what is the source?" I asked aloud, placing the cross absent-mindedly in my pocket.

"Source identified as Sample TSA-233-7A7 and Sample P303-019". The SR-FDA opened a hazard drawer. Double checking the various manifests we had, it was quickly discovered that the vial and the stopper were the culprits, so Zim and Michaels were forced to put away their new toys for the time being.

"Computer," I said again. "Exposure threat? Needed protocols?"

"Low levels of the following: Iodine-131, Tellurium-129m, Caesium-137, Strontium 90, various Plutonium isotopes: 15 terabecquerels total; exposure deemed limited – no organic protocol required".

Zim was already clacking away on his keyboard, running a directed scan at a molecular level to find out more about the vial and its vacant contents.

"All these were used in old Nuclear reactors. MoleScan shows a thin lead lining inside the vial, with Iodine-131, Tellurium-129m, Caesium-137, Strontium 90 ionization. This thing isn't radioactive itself, but it was built for at least minimal protection; short term transport most likely".

Zim popped up an enlarged hologram of the vial; with this magnification, we could see marks and scratches we'd missed before. Along one side, running lengthwise, we could make out some Japanese-looking script:

# 福島第一

"Computer – translate, please." I asked, pointing to the markings on the hologram.

The SR-FDA responded almost instantly. "Fukushima Daiichi".

# 4
## ❧Discovery❧

It had been nice having my Grandfather living with us. As great as it was for the girls to have him around, for me it was like a little slice of my own childhood had come back. As mom reminded me, that's not an opportunity that most people get, and we were all happy to see him up and puttering about. Of course, Granddaddy had started the family cooking tradition, so after a few months of his nightly meals, the week we'd just finished at work was undoubtedly going to help my waistline.

Despite my exhaustion, I spent the evening after dinner roughhousing with Erin and Olivia in the living room. We wore each other down until the girls were both too sleepy to argue about bedtime. I lifted

Erin gently from the living room floor, and carried her off to bed; just a few more steps, and the rest of the night – for however long I could stay awake – was mine to do with as I pleased. That was one of the big differences in my life since I had adopted the girls; before, I could come home, hop in the tub, relax, and fiddle about with whatever project I wished. Now, my time was their time, and the early baths and hours of reading, painting, or just plain old goofing off were relegated to the after bedtime slot. It really made me focus, and since I treasure any time spent with my girls, all the aspects of my life just seem more like sweet nectar now that time had become a bigger factor.

After I got Olivia into her jammies and tucked her in with her sister, I went back downstairs to gently wake Granddaddy. He kissed me on the cheek, muttering something about sleeping better in the armchair than he did in bed, and hazily stumbled off to his room for the night.

*"Nine pm"*, I said to myself with a smile as I clicked the downstairs lights off, *"and I've got everyone in bed except me, and tomorrow is Saturday. Time for Ellyandra!"*

\*\*\*\*\*\*\*\*

By the time I'd poured up a glass of Merlot, and made my way to my bedroom, the storm that had been threatening us all day had finally decided to unleash its fury against my apartment building, and despite being one hundred twenty five floors up, the pounding raindrops were just as intense, and the wind howled just as much as it did at ground level. *"This is perfect"* I thought to myself as I slid into my oversized tub, steam enveloping my body like silken robes. *"Wine, hot liquid relaxation, and the music of the storm; I'll sleep well tonight!"*

There is just something special about floating in the darkness, listening to the rain punish the walls and the wind whistle as it danced around the building. The warm water in my oversized tub was finally starting to make my shoulders release some of the tension they'd been storing up, and the wine was just starting to take its warmth from my belly to my brain. I sat up a little, leaning my head back on the side of the tub and placed a hot washcloth over my eyes. I could still see the flashes of lightning thru my closed eyelids. Strangely comforted by the added light show, I took the cloth from my eyes, opening them to reach for my wine, just in time to see the wall to one side of the tub illuminated again by the thunderbolts outside. But instead of a clear lighting of my bathroom wall – there was a shadow cast by the flash. I turned around abruptly, knocking the wineglass to the floor, and watched again as the flash outside illuminated the dark figure of a man on the impossible side of my window.

********

"You live on the 125$^{th}$ Floor, Ellie," Michaels said, looking out into the blackest midnight through my bathroom window. "Peeping Toms aren't usually a problem".

Before I could respond, Zim turned back to the window using his hand scanner. "I've got no displacement that would indicate that anything was attached to the window – so either they were hanging, or they were flying".

"Or she was half asleep and imagined it", I added, voicing what I was sure everyone was thinking. Their silence told me that's exactly what they were thinking, but neither one had the heart to say it first.

"It is possible, El," Zimmerman answered. "Happens to the best of us, especially as overworked as we've been".

Michaels was still tapping away on his handheld, quietly sipping his late night coffee. I'd called them instead of the regular police. I didn't want a house full of people waking up and worrying the girls. That's the last thing I wanted for them. Still, I had to call someone, and they both came over despite the hour and weather.

"OK, here we go, El," Michaels finally said, turning his handheld towards me. "Looks like it wasn't a dream after all. I hacked into the external building cameras. The camera from your building shows nothing, but the cameras on the top of the building next door showed this!"

On the small screen, through the rain, you could barely make out my building, and with that, the dark image of a figure floating next to the window. Fortunately the camera system was built to help track drones and transmit info to help keep them from flying into each other, so any flying movement bigger than the average bird was tracked, clarified and recorded by half the tall buildings in the county. The computer enhancements kicked in, and unblurred the dark image until you could clearly make out the figure of a man standing against my window, hovering on some kind of flying platform. The images were remarkably good given the situation, but even when he turned and flew away, there wasn't enough data to extrapolate his face.

\*\*\*\*\*\*\*\*

My granddaddy used to say that we needed a day between Saturday and Sunday, and that Monday's should be banned by international treaties. Despite my unsettled night, we all had a pretty good weekend. I didn't tell granddad or the girls about my peeping Tom; there was nothing they could do about it, and I didn't want them to be afraid. I did have Michaels download all the footage for further processing, and had a live feed set up to record any new high altitude visitors.

Monday was the day we'd planned on being able to finish the bulk of the work on the victim's from the plane crash. Most of the families had been contacted, and all but two had agreed to allow the bodies to be cremated, given the unknown process that had caused their skin and muscles to turn from flesh to stone. One of the one's we couldn't yet process was Passenger 303, not because the family had refused to allow cremation, but because we could locate no family.

"Zim," I called, sitting down at our shared workspace with a plop. "How are we coming on the rebuild for the plane?"

Zimmerman punched up a few screens on his terminal. "Looks like we're at 77 percent completion. We'll be ready by tomorrow morning".

"So until the build is finished, the Holo-system is free?" He nodded warily, cutting his eyes at me.

"Why?"

"Well, I was thinking; we can't do proper tissue slices or electron microscope work on the bodies because of their stone like state. Why not use a holographic lab to process Passenger 303? We could send everything through as though it was real, and the computer will bypass the limiting effects of the stone.

Zimmerman narrowed his eyes at me. "You really like taxing the system, don't you Ellie?" He turned around, half a smile poorly hidden on his face, and started pounding away on his keyboard. After a moment, he turned back and said, "You'll kill processing time by fifty two percent with a stunt like that, so it will be Wednesday, maybe even Thursday before the full plane simulation is viable. That being said, unless you bring down *your* simulation in the holo morgue, there should be no impact on the plane rebuild".

I reached over and hugged him. "You're the best Zimmerman! I'll head up to the holo morgue right now!"

"Give me five minutes Ellie," Zim said. "I have a feeling that you'll need some equipment called up that usually isn't in a holo morgue".

\*\*\*\*\*\*\*\*

The best we'd been able to get from any of the bodies was a skin scraping, and it had been like scraping calcium deposits off rocks. If we went too deep, or pressed too hard on the petrified flesh, pieces would break away, or crumble into dust. None of that dust had yielded us anything that was of use, so this was the last idea I could think of to get to the bottom of the porcelain death that had taken so many people.

Sure enough, despite some initial resistance to digesting the programming, the holographic samples taken from Passenger 303 were viable, and in short order I was finally looking at the skin cells from one of the victims.

"Hmm. Cell walls are all ruptured, but there are no signs of leakage of cellular fluids into the surrounding area." I adjusted the simulation of the electron scanner to zoom in on the nucleus of the cell I had pulled aside. "Chromosomal structure seems intact, but spectrographic analysis shows the material even at this level to have been replaced by inorganic material; minerals listed included kaolinite, feldspar, bone ash, steatite, and alabaster". I sat back, letting out a deep breath and hearing the 'click' of the incident recorder. I always talked to myself when studying things like this, so I figured I might as well record my notes at the same time.

"Computer, scan the sample for any residual traces of foreign bacteria". The Computer complied, and the lights in the holo morgue dimmed a bit, telling me I was pushing my luck. I crossed my fingers and waited. After a few minutes, the computer came back with an unexpected result. While bacteria were present, all the types were known and harmless - found practically on every living human. But just like the surrounding tissue, the bacteria had also been turned into inorganic structures.

I sat down and increased the magnification again on the simulated electron microscope, and again the lights dimmed - almost going out this time before a low level of lighting was restored. For the next hour, I slowly poured over every cellular structure in the sample, going nanometer by nanometer. I might as well have been looking at dust, with a drawing of a cell etched into the surface. Just as I was about to call it quits when I found myself scanning the rupture site in the cell membrane. There was something very out of place - a shape that looked like a tiny moon Lander. It was angular, with six 'legs' that extended down into the cell wall, and a 'head' at the top, formed in a dodecahedron.

"That's a virus," I said to myself, wanting a better view of the protein structure. When I tried to focus in on this object, the simulation cut the image.

"Computer, what caused the magnification failure?"

The computer quietly responded, "Simulation was rendered non viable due to projected isotopic activity that suggested a radioactive nature. The holographic nodes cannot simultaneously process both the position and projected movement of these isotopes due to the Heisenberg Uncertainty Principle."

The computer continued droning on with its science lesson, but at this point I wasn't listening. I was still trying to process what I'd seen. A radioactive virus? How was that possible? And how could it have had this kind of effect on every cell in the hosts' bodies?

\*\*\*\*\*\*\*\*

My discovery of the virus was only the beginning of the process. Michaels and Zimmerman both pooled their resources and started having all the available MR-CSA's rescan the body of Passenger 303. By the end of the day we were even more perplexed than we had been before. We now knew how the virus had affected all the organic structures in the hosts. The viral load was one to one; one virus for every cell in the body. That kind of load was unheard of, meaning the virus either had lain dormant until it was triggered, or reproduced itself at an incredible rate. Also, each of the 'calcified' viral structures exhibited a low level of radiation - the same radioactive signatures we'd discovered in the aluminum vial.

We had more questions now than when the investigation started and we'd had over three hundred victims to process. Now the makeshift morgue was pretty much emptied, and every fact we'd uncovered came with its own special set of new problems.

Granddaddy was right; Mondays should be outlawed.

## 5
### ❧Fate☙

Four days and hundreds of hours of combined processing time later, we still hadn't been able to take apart the virus to see how it ticked. In that same amount of time two more bodies, both victims of the *'Porcelain Death'* as the media was calling it, had been discovered between Mobile and Bay St Louis, MS. That gave us not only the planeload of people from the crash site in New Orleans, but three others spread across cities along Interstate 10, with no correlation we'd found so far.

By Friday, Zimmerman had spent an entire evening taking apart a SR-FDA, and rebuilding it from the ground up trying to get past the radiation protocols that kept shutting the analysis down. When he was done, we all marveled at the behemoth he'd made, and gasped in collective disappointment when it failed in a flurry of fumes and smoke.

At three o'clock, I went downstairs, changed into my workout clothes, and did a round of Kickboxing for a half an hour. I was just about to wind up my session when the comm terminal in the gym signaled an incoming call, so I grabbed my towel, and quickly dried my auburn curls so I would look presentable for whoever was calling me.

"Ello?" I asked, slightly out of breath.

"Mamma!" my girls said in stereo. "You look like a clown! Are you at a party?"

With the humidity, and my rapid towel strokes, my red hair had poofed out enough to make any clown jealous. "No party, my loves; just a workout". They both giggled as they held their Stuffed rabbit Chester up to the monitor.

"Chester thinks you look funny too!"

I smiled as I used my fingernails as a comb to try and bring some order to the chaos on top of my head. "You tell Chester that it takes funny to know funny," I answered with a smile. The girls made Chester throw his arms open in a hug, then they both started giggling again.

We chatted for another thirty minutes about their day, and how they wanted to go chasing butterflies this weekend. I promised them that my Mom and Granddad would take them, but I had some really important work to finish up here, so I'd be late. Of course, that led to the pouting phase (and if you've never seen a stuffed rabbit pout, you have truly missed one of life's miracle dramatic performances). Eventually, after promises had been made and cookies had been discussed, both my little ones perked right back up. Even Chester raised his ears when we talked about making carrot cookies just for him. I ended the call feeling more refreshed than I had in days. The silliness and joy that my girls brought to each day made me made feel alive and vibrant.

As well as my afternoon had gone, fate had other plans in store for me. I cleaned up the gym from my workout, and headed to the showers. While I stood under the never-ending hot water, clearing away the sweat and frustration of my workout, and the work week, I hit that almost meditative phase -

and I had a thought. My Aunt Michelle would have called it a 'vision', and maybe it was. But that doesn't mean it was a welcome one. It suddenly occurred to me who could help us, but be damned if I was going to be the one to ask him.

********

On Saturday morning, we were finally out of the deep freeze downstairs, and back in our regular workspaces on the 55th floor. As much as that was good news, we also had the joy of an enhanced build of the crashed plane in the holorecreator. I had indeed slowed the processing time, but it turns out that the plane build hit the same problem with virtual radiation that I'd run into, and Zim had to program around the issue to even complete the simulation. On top of it all, my Aunt Michelle was coming on Sunday to take Granddad and my girls to Mississippi for a few days, so I knew I would see them tonight, and then I could work through the weekend without having to worry.

We were about half an hour into the day, going over notes from the previous days and trying to get enough caffeine into our blood system to bring some life to our brains, when Director Forrest, my boss and head of the Mobile Regional Division, walked into my tiny office.

"Morning, everyone," Forrest said, shutting the door behind him. Usually he'd sported a shaved head, as many African-American males his age tended to do, but recently he'd started letting his hair grow back in, and there was black and grey fuzz on top of his head that made the little girl in me just want to rub it over and over again.

Forrest sat down in the only extra chair my small office had, which was fine since Zim was perched on the side desk near my coffee machine, and Michaels insisted on standing in the corner. Some people would have balked at having a meeting in such a confined space, but for us, it was like going on a long car ride with your brothers. It had its moments where you got on each other's nerves, or someone's choice of meals presented the enclosed area with that 'funny' smell, but overall it was a joy. Also, unlike the car ride, we could get out and explore any time, so that made it all the better.

"I got your message last night, Ellyandra," Forrest said, crossing his legs. "And I have to admit, I wasn't sure about making the call". I nodded as I passed my boss some fresh coffee, which he accepted with a nod before continuing. "That being said, I called Mr. McFarlane late last night, and he agreed to come in today to review the information". Forrest paused to sip on his coffee, and noticed the raised eyebrows on both Zimmerman and Michaels.

"He's the best qualified person in the country to continue your work, gentlemen".

"He's an ass," Michaels began, ignoring the hand Forrest had raised to stop him. "He's demeaning, selfish, arrogant, and just plain difficult to work with".

"He's also helped us solve cases in the past, *and* he's responsible for saving more than one life in this room, if you remember, Mr. Michaels". Forrest then turned to Zim, and asked, "Any feedback from you, Mr. Zimmerman?"

Zim nodded slowly, and quietly spoke. "He has the social skills of sour milk, Sir. But, he's one of the brightest people I've ever met".

Forrest finally turned to me, and asked "Your thoughts, Ellie?"

Like he had to ask. Forrest knew damn well why I'd rather not have Charles McFarlane brought on board for anything. Yes, he'd helped us in the past. And we knew him well. Hell, back in college he and I had been engaged, for crying out loud. And yes, he did save my life two years ago; probably saved other lives too. But in trying to help us last summer, he'd almost gotten me killed. Worse, my former fiancé's response to me adopting the girls couldn't even be classified as 'cool'; it was downright cold and cruel.

My boys had been with me, sitting in my study when he called and I told excitedly him about the girls. He and I had developed a friendship since he'd dropped back on the scene, and I wanted to share the joy with him. But as happy as I was, his tirade left me in tears, and after his last barrage of insults over the likes of *'something like me'* ever *thinking* about being a mother, I called him a 'rotten son of a bitch' and cut the transmission before he could have the pleasure of seeing me break down into uncontrollable sobs and self-doubt. I was so angry, so upset, that I couldn't even let my closest friends comfort me, and I knew beyond any doubt that was the real reason they didn't want him on board. But like it or not, I also knew that we needed him to unravel this virus, or it was going to keep killing more and more people. And I couldn't let my emotions get in the way of stopping it.

"Bring him on, Jim", I said quietly. The calm in my voice made Forrest look worried, but before he could even ask, I added, "but he needs to know that I am the boss here, and I will not find myself answering to him. It will be the other way around, or I will hand him his ass on a platter".

********

By the time we had finished our meeting, Charles had already gotten his credentials from the front desk, and was down in the Bio-tank where we usually handled **potential bio-hazards and other dangerous materials.** I hated it down there, especially knowing that the emergency protocols had once been overridden and my boys and I had almost been gassed into oblivion. As far as I was concerned, if Charles could find an answer to help us unlock this thing, that was fine. *'Maybe we could gas him afterwards,'* the little deamon in my head added, but I shrugged it off knowing full well that I didn't mean that, and headed to the holorecreator with Zim and Michaels to finally get some 'hands on' time with the crashed plane.

# 6
## ❧Ghosts❧

I don't think any of us knew exactly what to expect when the doors to the Holorecreator were opened. All the scans had been made after the plane was raised, so we wouldn't be faced with a snapshot filled with floating corpses and debris. Still, even with my memories of the plane mostly being the events that took place beneath the waves, the pure ghastliness of the scene couldn't be understood until the water had drained away, leaving crumpled bodies, stained with the residue of the lake water, algae and decay, amid the wreckage of the once stunning X-999. Fortunately, Zimmerman had already turned off scent reproduction, and had also compensated for the angular displacement the fuselage had bent into after the crash, so we weren't barraged with the smell of the lake water, nor were we fighting our way up and downhill.

Michaels stopped to look at one of the passengers seated close by. "This could take hours, Ellie". He reached out with his hand, clad tightly in holo-reactive Ferrin, and gentle tried to move the body. It responded as though it were stone. Almost everybody we'd processed had initially been in a sitting position, and Tuttle's crew had broken almost every single one of them trying to force them into a more traditional laying position. I was unendingly grateful that the majority of the families involved had allowed cremation; it kept them from ever having to know the full extent of the damage their loved ones went through, even after death.

"Tag out everyone except the flight crew, and passenger 303, Aaron," I ordered. Michaels hit a few buttons on his handheld and the passengers vanished. "Zim, head up to the cockpit with me. Michaels, you look for 303 and get some images of his position. I want to know what he was up to, if we can".

Michaels nodded and started his pass through the behemoth of an airplane. Zimmerman and I walked down the main aisle of the first level, consciously trying to avoid the photonic seats that we instinctively knew we *could* walk through. One learned quickly in a Holorecreator that if you pretended that everything wasn't really there, the full body Ferrin suites would *remind* you in unpleasant and sometimes painful ways that you were supposed to be reacting, and interacting, in a realistic way.

The planes' image was still crunched up, and the cockpit was smashed in like an accordion.

"Computer, remove the plane body and wreckage in this cell; by stages, please. We need to see the crew". Slowly, the computer complied, and layers of metal and fiberglass gave way to layers of electronics and wiring, until finally the bodies of the Captain and his co-pilot were visible. They barely looked human in this crushed state, but one thing I noticed almost instantly was that their skin didn't have the same glossy look the other bodies had exhibited.

"What do you think, Zim?"

He grabbed his handheld and started coding away. "I'm piping the full image up to the holo morgue. And Ellie,"

"Yes?" I asked, waiting for Zim to finish.

"There's no trace of radiation in this scan. These men are clean".

\*\*\*\*\*\*\*\*

After we'd finished in the cockpit of the plane, we headed back up the main aisle, and up the stairs to the second level. We all knew we'd never left the floor, but the holorecreator did a fantastic job of screwing with your perceptions. You could have been standing right next to someone, and as long as the power levels held, you'd never know it.

We found Michaels in the top level, back behind the bathroom, and standing next to Passenger 303, who was lying on the floor, leaned up against a ventilation grate. On the floor lay an open tin filled with a white, powdery substance. Stuck to the open grate was a plastic baggie, half-filled with the same white powdery substance, and right next to that, suspended on a wire loop and hook, was the uncorked vial.

"What the Hell?" I questioned, reaching toward the vial and 'removing' it. As I moved it, the computer once again announced "RADIATION

WARNING", and then the image of the vial vanished from my hands.

"I think I see what happened here Ellie," Michaels began, pausing to say, "Computer, re-initialize the image of the vial, remove any radiation signatures, and begin simulation MICHAELS 303-001".

The vial re-appeared, once again connected to the ventilation grid by its makeshift small wire loop and hook. Michaels pointed to the plastic bag and its mushy, once powdery substance. "Computer, dry out the substance in the bag, and initiate simulated ventilation". The computer complied, and the once again powdery substance began to flow out of the bag, and right across the open vial, into the vent system.

"Now, imagine that there was more to this substance; image the bag was full. That would be more than enough to spread through a plane like this, and deliver whatever this is to everyone on board".

"Everyone except the Cabin crew," Zim added. "The cockpit is on an isolated airflow system".

"That's why we didn't detect the radiation signature in their cockpit", I commented out-loud, seeing only quiet nods of acknowledgement.

"If that's the case, then whatever killed the flight crew in the cockpit was independent of this damned virus", Michaels surmised. "Otherwise, their remains would have had a low-level rad signature, and been fossilized as well".

The three of us were just turning to head back to the cockpit when the lights dimmed again, but this time pieces of the holographic walls around us started falling down, vanishing in a flash before they hit the floor. We watched the entire simulation disappear before our eyes, layer by layer, until all that was left was the three of us, standing in the now empty holorecreator, looking bewildered.

********

"What do you mean, it's gone, Zim?" I asked as Zim sat in his cubicle, frantically looking for the scan files of the plane.

"The files just aren't there anymore, Ellie. It looks like someone deleted them during the simulation."

I let out a loud groan in frustration. In order to rebuild the simulation, we'd have to requisition Tuttle's office in the TSA for the original files, which of course would make us look like damned fools. "Who in the Hell has clearance to delete files at this level of the system? I thought it was a secured network?"

Zim was stammering, checking every protocol, and coming up empty-handed. "Director Forrest can delete simulation files, and you can delete them as long as you have an additional level 2 code to go along with yours".

Just then, my old fiancé Charles McFarlane walked into the room, munching on a candy bar and staring intently at a display page. A wrenching feeling in my gut told me that we may have just found our culprit.

"Hi, Charlie," I said as he passed by.

He stopped mid-step and cringed, crying out "You know I hate that nickname, Ellie".

I ignored his protest and playfully skipped over to him. "Question for ya, 'Mr. McFarlane'".

Putting my arm around his shoulder, I walked him over to Zim's cubicle where he and Michaels could witness the impending beating I was planning on giving my old beau. "Do you happen to know, by any chance, if you deleted anything from our network today?"

"Yea, I needed more drive-space," he answered nonchalantly. "I couldn't overwrite some note files on the main drive I'd been given access to, so I backed up what I needed, pulled the drive, and flattened it".

Zim was about to come out of seat, but I held my arm out to stop him. "And what, pray tell, did you do with these backups? Hmmmm?"

Charles finally started putting two and two together, and asked, "What? Are you guys angry about something?" He reached into his pocket and pulled out a small, portable drive. "I backed everything up on this," he said, holding it out to us. Zimmerman was just starting to breathe a sigh of relief what Charles added, "Well, almost everything. One really big file-set was in use, so I had to dump that". With this news, Zim started getting almost teary-eyed, and I could tell that Michaels was just about to lose his composure when Charles added,

"But I think I've got the root of this virus figured out".

\*\*\*\*\*\*\*\*

Charles took us to the holo-morgue he'd been using all morning, and sat down at the control console. In the air around us, samples of cells began to appear, each one with the virus attached near a rupture point in the cell wall.

"I know you all think I'm a genius for figuring this out so fast," Charles said smugly, "and you're right; but if I am to be honest, I saw the precursor to this virus a few years ago when we were going through Old Man Waldorf's research".

"OK, and just what does that drooling son of a bitch have to do with this, Charles?" I asked as nicely as I could.

"Well, while I was going through papers and studies from his 'extended' lab circuit, I came across something he'd personally been working on for the military. Apparently, his place in Oslo was where he did most of this research, and he'd made good progress for years, until he hit a stopping point that even his best people couldn't get around. I needed the drive-space to translate the original research files once I found them, and I've started some of my own decryption programs, but since this virus is active it would seem that someone else not only found the research, but figured out the problems and finished the viral design".

Zim and Michaels studied his work, completely forgetting that Charles had stopped us in the middle of our investigation by virtue of his self-centeredness. As my boys talked about the implications of this information, I walked behind the desk and leaned over, quietly whispering in Charles' ear, "Nice work Charlie; don't you *ever* delete anything off my network again without permission, or I swear I'll have you hanging by your ears next time. Got it?"

Charles looked up at me, giving a small nod, and then turned back to discuss the progress with Michaels and Zimmerman. Charles had always had more than a little disdain for Michaels, but Aaron was catching on, and showing his knowledge in ways that Charles could appreciate. So despite his demeaning comments and the pedestal he put himself on, the three of them soon started actually making headway together.

"How'd they figure out the correct signature was **Fukushima**? That place is a forty year old wreck!" Zim kept adding up data on his handheld, puzzling over the process.

"Maybe it was just the luck of the draw," Aaron added. "How many radioactive wastelands do people really have to choose from?"

Charles jumped in, adding "I'd expect that answer from you, Monkeyboy. Any really intelligent person wouldn't be looking for what they need, would they? They'd *make* the signature they needed. Or, they'd build the virus to a type of radiation they had easy access to. Besides, I've already run a simulation on the projected structure of the delivery powder, and the radiation signature from the Fukushima sample only caused the virus to become active forty seven percent of the time".

The boys continued their discussion, and after a while, Charles looked over to me and smiled, just a little. In that moment, I wondered if he even knew I was still angry with him. Or if he even realized I was angry or hurt to begin with.

Then I wondered why I would even care.

# 7
## ❧Dinner❧

Despite working together all day, we had all planned on heading over to Zim's place on Dauphin Island for dinner that night. The girls' loved going to Zimmerman's underwater apartment, and every time we went to visit, they'd bring books about the ocean, and goggles for 'just in case'. Even Chester the stuffed rabbit got in on the act, putting on his best swim trunks and donning a snorkel.

Normally, Erin and Olivia were great at getting ready to go somewhere; but it seemed that their excitement was getting in the way, and my own scatter-brained tendency to forget things was definitely starting to show in them both. After forty-five minutes, we *finally* got out of the house, I loaded us all into Deloris (who'd had her AI transferred to a larger vehicle after I adopted the kids), and off we went to the remains of the Island.

My granddad used to say that driving to the island would ruin a good hour or more, and despite the higher speeds allowed due to the traffic control programs in the vehicles, it still felt like it took forty forevers to get out there. Deloris was more than happy to have all of us together, holding two conversations at once – one with the girls about their underwater destination, and one with me about how busy I'd been, how things were with the girls, etc. The vehicles' AI had developed greatly since the girls had entered our lives, and riding with Deloris had become something of a treat.

There wasn't much left of Dauphin Island anymore; really, it was just a patch of sand at the end of the bridge, with a few buildings remaining above ground. It was the apartment towers that went deep under the water that made this place special, and the views of life in the Gulf of Mexico were more than relaxing – they were awe inspiring.

The boys had been kind enough to delay the meal for our arrival, so dinner was ready and waiting by the time we got there. As usual, Zim had made quite a spread; there was spaghetti and bread, garlic butter and parmesan cheese for us all. They also had tea and juice for the girls and for the adults there was beer and wine almost without end. My girls fit in perfectly with the boys, and meals like this were just a reminder to me that, while I may have lost some free time and personal freedom when I adopted them, I'd only enhanced every other aspect of my life.

After the meal was done, and the girls helped the apartment cleaning system by getting all the plates and glasses to the kitchen, they settled down in Zim's living room in front of his big picture window, and turned on the outside spotlights so they could start 'fish spotting' in the dark gulf waters. I knew they'd be at it as long as I let them, so the boys and I sat on the opposite end of Zim's living room, sipping wine, and trying to de-stress from the huge amount of work we'd had on us for weeks. Aaron started telling jokes (kid friendly, because the girls were always listening), and we finally started relaxing a bit when Zim's doorbell rang. We all raised our eyebrows a bit, waiting for Zim to find out who was visiting. I don't think any of us were happily surprised when Charles McFarlane turned out to be the late guest.

Charles had an armload of digital papers and boxes of data cards, almost dropping them as he pushed past Zimmerman and entered the home. "OK, my first round of simulations finished an hour ago, so you need to see what I've come up with so far".

Zim slowly shook his head and calmly closed the door behind the unwelcomed guest, as Charles pushed items around on Zim's coffee table and started unloading his information.

"Charlie," I softly said, setting my wine glass down directly on a stack of his papers. "How did you know we'd all be here?"

He looked at me blankly, and answered "Zim and the other one were talking about it earlier, so here I am".

I was trying to not get angry in front of my girls, who were still playing at Zim's window. "And did you even wait to be invited in, Charlie? I know your mother taught you better manners. You didn't even apologize for being late".

Charles puffed up a bit, rebutting "Why say the obvious, Ellie? And he *was* holding the door for me".

Zim interjected himself into the fray, asking, "Do you want any wine, Charles? I guess I don't mind another guest". I knew this was Zim's way of keeping the peace, and I wasn't about to be disrespectful to my friend in his own home, so I gently picked up my glass, and let the matter drop.

I sat and watched the boys go over Charles' results, drinking in the data silently, not adding or questioning anything. They all knew that, despite appearances, I was catching every word they said. The science was anything but above my head; I could hold my own with any of them, even the all mighty

Charles McFarlane. When they started rehashing arguments, I figured I had all the info I needed for the time being, so I got up from the sofa, and walked over to the window, sat down next to my girls, and asked, "How goes it, my loves?"

"We're good, Mamma," Erin answered, trying to suppress a yawn. "We found lots of pretty fishes, and stuff. 'Livia decided to drawn them for you!"

Olivia lay belly down on the floor, facing the now-dark window, with a stack of crayon-coloured paper on one side, and fresh paper on the other. Chester was right up by the glass, so he could get a 'good look' at all the fish.

"Did you do all these, my sweet girl?" I asked, picking up the stack of paper, and shuffling through the childlike renditions of redfish, rays and other things I couldn't begin to identify.

"Uh-huh, sure did," Olivia answered, still intently colouring away on her latest project. "But this is my last'n tonight, Mamma; I'm gettin' tired".

I raised my glass for another small sip, but stopped dead as I shuffled to the next drawing. In between all the fish and such, Olivia had drawn a diver.

"Livy, honey?" I tried to suppress the gulp in my throat, "Why did you draw a diver here, my love?"

"Oh, he's nice Mamma" Olivia, answered. "He waved at me and Erin, and even Chester!"

"Aaron. Zim." I called over calmly, not wanting to upset my girls. Charles gave an exasperated *harrumph* at being interrupted by children, but the boys both got right up and came over, each suppressing a strong reaction as I held out the drawing for them to see.

"Didn't Livy do good, Mr. Zim?" Erin asked, holding up a second drawing with the diver.

"She did a lovely job, hon," Zim answered. "Excuse me just a moment, girls". Zim went into his kitchen and hit his comm terminal to contact Apartment Security.

"How long ago did you see this man, Olivia?" Aaron asked, gently kneeling down at her side.

"Oh, he came by a couple times".

I turned around and gazed out into the inky blackness of the underwater night. "You had to be using the spotlights to see him, didn't you?"

Just about that moment, Zim's call to Security took effect, and the buildings' exterior lights came on, flooding the area outside practically in daylight. And right on the other side of the glass, staring me in the face the whole time, was the nameless diver. I jumped, and the girls screamed at his sudden appearance. Before we could react the man jetted away using a handheld transport to shoot himself through the water.

"Damn it!" I cried, stomping my foot on the floor. "First someone's watching me in my bathroom, and now the creep is following me to my friend's house for a peek!" I clenched my fist and yelled, "This is *really* starting to piss me off!"

Charles had finally gotten up from the living room to join us, and came to stand next to me, looking out to the shrinking form of the diver off in the distance. "Well, Ellie, look on the bright side," he said quietly. "Maybe it's not the same creep. Maybe you have two stalkers instead".

"That is not actually comforting, Charlie," I answered, kneeling down to hug my girls tight. "Not comforting at all".

# 8
## ❧Arguments❧

I spent Sunday alone in the lab, working off more than a little frustration. I have never liked being followed; especially not when the person following me could apparently not only swim, but fly as well. Granddad and the girls were gone until Monday evening, so I locked up tight at home, grabbed some extra clothes, and headed to my office. Charles had left a pile of notes and records on my desk for review, which had to have irked him beyond measure. He hated oversight of any kind. Most people thought that was because he was a super genius, but I knew it was because in reality, he was a scared little boy, who was terrified of being seen making a mistake.

Despite the evidence we had, the virus was still considered a theory; we had no evidence to show that what we'd found could cause the type calcification and mineralization of living tissue that had killed all our victims. Plus, even if we were right, until we understood the how's and why's, we had no way of fighting the virus; that part is what really scared me. Something this deadly, and this gruesome, had to be stopped.

After several hours of matching up notes with samples, and pouring over technical information that pushed my limits, I did start to see a definable pattern. The fact that old Reginald Waldorf's company had been involved in the initial development of this virus was unsettling at best. The man had not only mass murdered more than twelve thousand people over a period of forty years, he'd also been responsible for the crippling mental degradation of his own son, all in the name of his twisted version of science. On top of that, he'd used my Grandfather's friendship as a tool to ultimately kidnap and experiment on an Uncle I'd never been able to know, and even tried to kill me. Anything that even suggested his fingerprints was considered taboo, yet here we were fighting his madness once again.

********

Time does funny things to you when you get so focused on a given train of thought. I'd been going through Charles' work so intently that, when people started showing up for work Monday morning, at first I thought it was just the cleaning staff. Before I knew it, I'd been awake for well over thirty-six hours, and Michaels and Zimmerman were both in their usual places in my office catching up on my weekends' work.

"Ellie," Zim started, slowly sipping his coffee. "I see why you made these nucleotides merge here; I just don't see *how* you explain it happening."

"Go to page 177 of the dataflow sheet, and check sub-section 12. That shows how the inert material is changed at a sub-atomic level in the nucleotide chain when exposed to the correct radioactive signature". I put my head down on my desk as the boys kept going.

"This goes beyond McFarlane's work, Ellie. You should be proud". Michaels said, setting down his handheld and going to the coffee machine.

"Too damn tired to be proud," I murmured, not lifting my head off my desk. "Plus, now that my need for sleep is catching me, I'll need all three of you to go over the work; make sure I didn't miss anything".

"You really want us to bring him in to review your work, El?" Zimmerman asked. "You know he'll find a way to tear it up, and then redo it in his own style so he can own it".

"Don't care," I hazily responded, lifting my noggin just a tad to peer through my bright red curls. "Oversight is mandatory. Everything in those files is theoretical, until we can show it in practice".

Just as I was saying this, my office door opened, and in strode Charles McFarlane. "Damn right it's theoretical, Ellie!" I let my head fall back to the desktop as he continued. "Just want do you think you're doing, tinkering with my work? You said you wanted notes to review, not notes to take apart and put back together in some weird, hapless, cyclopean jigsaw".

Both Zim and Michaels started to verbally tear into Charles, but I raised a hand (still without raising my head) and somehow brought silence to the room. "I'm too damn tired for this, boys. Zim, *you* take the research we have so far and cross check it in the computer systems. I want every simulation possible run by five tonight. Aaron, I want *you* to take *Mr.* McFarlane, get him set up in a clean lab with all materials available, and get him running real time test with live materials; we'll either prove or disprove this virus theory".

Both my boys responded with 'Sure thing, Ellie' and were off in a flash. Charles, however, stood in front of my desk, silent and waiting. Finally, after a minute or so, he said, "This conversation isn't done yet, Ellyandra". With this, he turned to leave, slamming my door behind him.

********

It's amazing how a few hours of sleep on a hard desk will bring out the best in you. Not only does your face stick to the desk, but the headache you wake up with is usually nothing less than a screamer. I woke around three o'clock in the afternoon, feeling like death that had only slightly been warmed over, and clawed my way towards consciousness. *'This is why the boys got me my own coffee machine'* I thought to myself as I reached over and filled my cup. Zim still had two hours to get me the needed simulations, and I knew that if I offered a hand, he'd try to do more than could really be done in that timeframe, so I hopped downstairs to the gym showers, cleaned up, and went to find Aaron and Charlie, to see what progress they'd made.

I found Aaron in the bio-tank down in the sub-levels, working with gloved hands to handle some of the evidence from the crash.

"What's up?" I asked quietly, my head still reminding me that oak does not a good pillow make.

"Well, I figured out how they got a radioactive substance past security to get it on the plane", Michaels said, pulling his hands out of the gloves. "That prosthetic leg? The empty chamber was custom built to fit the vial from Fukushima. And the leg chamber was lead lined – when closed, it would look just like any other medical device on a full body scan".

"Damned ingenious".

"And insidious. Whoever was behind this knew exactly what they were up to, right down to the last man, who had his own leg cut off so he could wear the prosthesis".

"Show me," I said, sitting down at a nearby terminal and pulling up the holo-scan of passenger 303. Sure enough, the cross-section of the amputation site showed at most three months of healing in the bone; the actual skin that covered the stump was set together with a protein 'glue', and all the major nerves leading to that area of the skin had been severed.

"Plus, I discovered that we have an untainted sample of the virus," Aaron said, walking over to me and setting down the water-logged sample of white powder that Tuttle had sent from the plane wreckage.

"Hey!" I shouted, nearly falling out of my seat trying to get distance between me and the sample. "What the hell are you trying to do?!"

Aaron chuckled, reaching out a hand to steady me. 'No worries, Ellie. This is what I was testing when you came in. I've taken this and exposed it to the radiation from the vial. Either what we have is too low level to activate the virus, or sitting in Lake Pontchartrain caused enough damage to make it inert. Either way, we're safe".

I stood up, grabbing the small metal container with the white powdery substance, and threw the lid on it. "And since it's safe to leave the bio-tank, this is going upstairs to little Charlie McFarlane. Let him see if he can recreate this in a more pure form".

Working my way up the stairs from the bio-tank was good exercise, and before I knew it, the combination of caffeine and the aerobic workout that the stairwells provided had cleared my head from its pounding misery. When I finally approached the door to the lab that Charles had been assigned, I started to just bounce right in, but I stopped myself. I knew I was intentionally egging him on, and I knew why. There was something in me that, even though we'd broken up years ago, still wanted his friendship; hell, still wanted his approval, even though I knew I didn't need it. As angry as I was with him, I was the one poking the hornet's nest, just to get back at him, in some small way. And I either hadn't realized it, or hadn't allowed myself to admit it until that very moment. So, instead of just hammering my way in, I stopped and knocked instead.

"hmmmph" was the only answer I received, so I twisted the knob and went in. Charles was sitting on the far side of the room, face buried in a holo-scope. He didn't even look up when he said, "Get some rest, Ellie?"

"Yea, I'm good now. Thanks". I answered, calmly setting down the metal container. "We found a sample of the original virus; thought you might be able to use it".

"'M'kay". Charles grunted, still not looking up. I could see that, in the back corner of the room, he'd hooked up a modified MR-CSA to a small isolation unit, and it was running some process on a sample of material.

"What'chya got, Charlie?" I asked, not catching his hated nickname in time to keep it from coming out of my mouth.

"You should know. It's your protocol, Ellyandra". He only used my full name when he was pissed off, which used to make me take a back step. But today, here and now, it just made me angry again.

"Do you even know why Director Forrest called you, Charlie?" I asked, more sneer in my voice than I'd expected.

"Uh, yeah. And here I am working on it. What do you want? An award for finally admitting you couldn't do this without me?"

Before I could answer, Charles switched off his holoscope and slid down from his workstation, walking closer to me. He wasn't threatening, but the tension in his gate was evident. "You couldn't get this far on your own. Zim knows computers, but he can only simulate what you can devise. Michaels is a walking testosterone pill with a meager mind, and you... you just take what they can give you and hope for the best".

I felt my eyes tearing up, and I could feel the top of my head getting hot. "You, of all people, have no right to judge us, Charles". I spoke slowly, purposefully, to try and convey my growing ire before it got the best of me. In my mind's eye, I was already kicking the crap out of him, as I had off and on for years.

"Really, Ellie? Why not? After three years, without a word, you drop back into my life needing help, and what did I do? I helped you; saved your life if I remember. And you know what? Things were nice after that. At least we were friends again".

"You and I remember that *very* differently; When you and I split, I told you to 'give me a call once you found out that you weren't God', and I'd meant it. I only came to you on the Waldorf case because we needed your understanding of the medical science involved".

"I still saved your life, Ellie"

"I didn't ask you to, Charlie". I shot back, only growing angrier because I knew he was right.

"Then last year, you nearly ruined my symposium. That must've made you feel great, to try and belittle me in front of a roomful of people".

"Belittle you?" I exclaimed. "You never needed my help to make an ass of yourself, Charles. We were discreet and appreciative; even though you almost got us killed".

"Hardly my fault, Ellie". Charles responded, now pacing back and forth in front of me. "I seem to recall telling you that I didn't trust those men, but it was the only 'in' that I had access to. You knew it, and you took the chance. Your call, *not* mine!"

"Then what about the girls?" I said, the truth for my anger finally making its way to the surface. "You knew I always wanted kids, and when I told you, when I wanted to share something that special with you, despite all the disappointments and all the hurt between us – when I called *you* to share in the joy, all you did was insult me! Call them little brats, call me a fool for thinking I could ever be a mother. *How \*dare\* you* ever expect me to *even toy* with having a reason to be kind to you!"

Charles' jaw dropped, and his face contorted into a twisted frown. "Is that what this is all about? After all the shit you and I have been through, and it's those girls that get you so angry?"

Charles turned away from me, stomping back to his holoscope, and pretended to go back to his work. He knew he'd pushed me to that point; the point where calm and reasonable discussion was done, where logical thought was set aside and pure, raw emotion was boiling over in an uncontrollable cascade of thoughts and feelings. He also knew that he couldn't just walk away; he knew I wouldn't let him.

I slid up next to his workstation, sticking my face into his personal space. "No Charles, it's you that gets me that angry!" I slammed my hand down on the workstation next to the holoscope, asking "Why won't I be a good mother, Charlie? Out of all the years you've known me," I continued ranting as I moved to his right side, "what excuse, what reason did I ever give you to say such a horrible, hateful thing to me? Come on, Charlie, tell me why?"

"BECAUSE THEY'RE NOT MINE!" he screamed at me, turning around to look me directly in the face. I could now see his own eyes were tearful and red. "You would have been a great mother – for OUR kids! But no, that possibility, you didn't even think of it, did you?"

I was stunned. I was literally stunned, unable to respond or even to think. I found that, while the heat of the anger was still upon me, and the tears were still flooding from my eyes, the anger itself had taken a backseat, and I stood there, trying to remember how to even form the words that I couldn't think to say.

"Charles…" I started, but he cut me off.

"Don't call me Charles; not you."

I tried to relax a little; my shoulders released some of the tension that they'd been housing. "Charlie, I … don't know what to say".

Charles took his lab coat sleeve and wiped his own eyes, then reached out to gently wipe the tears away from mine. "Nothing to say, Ellie".

It was at this moment that the lights in the room shut down, replaced with red hazard lighting. The MR-CSA in the corner was almost at a meltdown point; it had been working too long beyond its operating limits. The last thing it announced before it hit total system failure was "Porcelain Death Virus recreated: stable at 99% of original…"

# 9
## ~Subterfuge~

Usually, when I let Deloris drive us home, I'm either still working on paperwork, or too tired to let myself drive. This time, I was simply still too worked up to think straight. The Artificial Intelligence in Deloris' programming somehow knew that this was not a normal state of being for me, and she drove herself and me home in silence, only speaking to wish me a good night's rest when she dropped me off.

"How could he *possibly* even think..." I started saying to myself, watching the lift doors open through a mental fog. "And why take that out on me? On the girls?" I turned to the glass side of the lift and watched the city lights move as it slowly crawled up the side of the building to level 125. The city was just coming to life in the darkening sky, lights calling and shining bright, and people gathering 'round them. I was just about to get lost in the twinkling sparkles when the lift came to an abrupt stop and the lighting inside shut down. The jolt knocked me to the floor, causing me to hit my head on the handle of the emergency call box. I opened the box to find the comm system was dead – no power at all. The meter inside the box showed that I was almost to floor 125, so I took the emergency key out of its storage place, and unlocked the doors, forcing them open just enough to wiggle through and hopefully up to floor level.

Some of the emergency lighting had kicked in, giving me an idea of where to place my footing as I struggled to get up and out of the lift. I was halfway there when the sounds of boots started coming from the nearby stairwell, and I let myself fall back into the car just as the door opened. This was one of those moments when being tiny was a blessing, and I crunched my small frame as tight as I could into the corner of the lift. In the darkness, I could barely see the silhouetted figures of armed men walking past the partially opened door. One of the men stopped and set his searchlight into the lift, its silken beam missing my legs only by half an inch, but I was somehow safe in the blanket of shadow, and soon the men continued down the hallway. Once they had passed, I was able to escape the car.

Setting my pulser from sound to electric stun, I felt like I was in one of Granddaddy's old video games as I quietly crept down the darkened hallway. At this floor, there were only a few homes on each level, and it didn't take me long to figure out that this group of ruffians were headed to *my* apartment. *'Bad luck for them'* I thought to myself. My girls and I had been all over this floor, and even though there were only a few halls between the apartments, there were still janitor's closets, server rooms, and all sorts of nooks and crannies that these idiots didn't know about, and I planned to use every one of them to my advantage.

Then it hit me –Granddaddy and my girls would be home by now! The very idea of them being assaulted by these men made me ill at first, but that quickly changed to anger. There was no way I'd let these *things* lay a finger on my girls if I had anything to say about it. I worked my way across the floor to the server room, and used my Federal access key to unlock the coded door. Once inside, it was easy to use a maintenance terminal to pull up the internal cameras and see that the group had only posted one guard at my door. The comm system had been disabled, so I set the data-stream to not only record, but to pipe the info through the net to Michaels and Zimmerman. Once I knew that backup would be on the way, I set out to sneak my way towards my own home. With my pulser set to electric, I came up behind the lone guard at my door, and brought him down quickly and quietly. I'd say painlessly, but having been hit with one of these before, I knew the feeling was anything but painless. I used some quick-ties on his hands and feet, took away his weaponry, and grabbed his headset from his unconscious body. As I secured him and took his equipment, I realized that his outfit seemed familiar, like something maybe from an old movie, but I couldn't place it.

Shrugging it off, I placed his headset on and made my way silently into my home. I could hear them talking, using very thick, Eastern European accents.

"Kitchen is clear," one voice said. "Dmitri, search the study. Yalow, Kason, head upstairs. Kill anyone but the girl".

Hearing this, I slid into my study before Dmitri could get there; it was close to the front door, and all too easy in the dark to hide just inside the doorway. I flattened him before he knew what hit him. A few more quick-ties, disarm another one – piece of cake, right?

One day I'll learn to keep thoughts like that *out* of my internal dialogue; fate always seems to prove me wrong. Something I learned a long time ago was, no matter how great your advantage, never get cocky. Karma has a tendency to find ways to smack you around when you do. Despite the fact that this was my own home, which I knew well with or without light, my advantage was not as strong as I thought. I worked my way into the living room, and saw two shadowy figures at the top of my stairs. They also saw me, and each took a shot, one bullet nicking my upper right arm. I raised my pulser, and with two quick shots, both men were down, but that was all the power left in the weapon. It was just down to me, and one other man, who was well armed, and thanks to all the noise, had to know I was here.

*"Hide me, Mamma!"* I could hear Erin saying in my memory. She and Olivia had found so many hiding places it was astounding. I turned around, aimlessly at first, then started to find my way thru the shadows, pulser held uselessly in my hands, thinking

*"So where over here would my girls hide? Where is this guy?"* I worked my way to the bottom of the stairs, when I almost tripped over something. Placing my back to the wall, I reached down to grab whatever had made me stumble; it was a pair of military boots. My uninvited guest had apparently tossed aside his shoes so he could sneak up on me better. I laughed to myself as I stared out into the shadowy living room, just waiting for what was inevitable. If there was one thing I knew to look for in my home, it was action figures, craft items, and building bricks.

"čurák!" I heard from a dark corner of the living room. That's all I needed to know where to jump my prey and attack, and attack I did. I tore into the dark figure with all the rage of a mother lioness defending her cubs. Punches landed, missed and landed again in the dark as we fought. The lights started to come on, flickering in and out, and I thought, *"My boys will be here any second!"* Until then, I was face to face with a very large, albeit barefoot, man. My initial attack had placed me on top of him, and as I'd landed blow after blow, riding his shoulders like a buffalo, he struggled to get hold of me enough to throw me off him. He'd dropped his rifle when I jumped him, but once I was no longer on top of him, he more than made up for the ground he'd lost by pulling a large knife.

Kickboxing at a knife fight wasn't a strong tactic, but being my mother's child, and knowing far too well the advantage of having proper home decor, I jumped back towards the mantle, and grabbed an old Calvary sword from its display, swooshing it in front of me like Robin Hood.

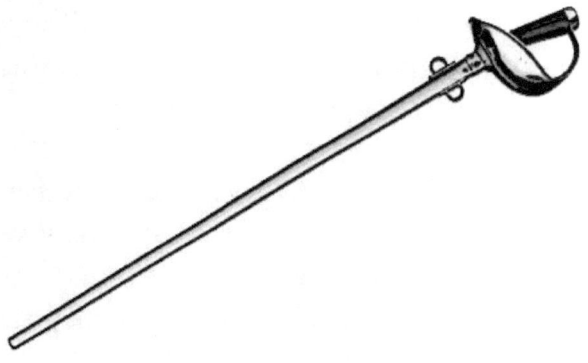

Remember what I said about cockiness, and Karma? It hadn't occurred to me, as I sized up the number of invaders in my home, that one or more had been silent on their radio. I immediately realized this when a huge set of arms wrapped around me from behind, putting me in a lock so tight that I dropped my sword.

"Získať je odtiaľto!" barked the man who held me. The barefoot man ran up and grabbed one of the unconscious troops from the top of my stairs and carried him out.

"So, we have our prize at last," the man said, his thick Slavic accent almost too strong to understand. "You have a meeting, child".

"You know what else I have?" I asked.

"A bad attitude?" he answered smugly.

"No, a heel!" I cried, putting all the power I could into a reverse groin kick that not only caused him to release me, but to drop to the floor wailing in pain.

Finally free of his grip, I turned around to defend myself just as Michaels, Zimmerman and Forrest entered the room, followed by a dozen policemen. The man turned, saw them with pulsers drawn, and slammed his mouth shut with such force we heard a crack. Seconds later, he fell over dead.

I didn't have time to care. Now that I was free, I had to find my girls. Bolting through my home, I searched every dust bin, every closet, every chute and tube that could be used by a little girl to hide or escape, but neither my grandfather, nor my twins were anywhere to be found.

I ran back to my study where one of the intruders I'd flattened was still out cold, and hit my comm terminal to bring it back online after the power loss. The welcome screen took what felt like an eternity to finally finish loading, and I almost passed out when I saw there was a message waiting for me; granddad had taken the girls out to a movie, and they'd be home late.

My family was safe. For now, at least.

## 10
### ❧Flashback❧

"If you wanted us to come over for a party Ellie," Michaels said, waving one of the policemen to the location of another unconscious attacker, "you could have invited better company".

I sat on the sofa in my living room, rubbing a sore spot on my ribs from the little jaunt I'd just taken. "But then where would the surprise be?" I asked, wincing just a little when I drew in my next breath. "Besides, I'm not the one who planned this shindig".

Forrest was pacing around every room, looking for anyone we may have missed, or anything that may have been left behind. After no less than five sweeps thru each floor, he was finally convinced that my home was secure.

"Damn it, Ellyandra, why didn't you tell me that you were being followed?" he asked, sitting down in a wing chair next to the sofa. "You could have been kidnapped, killed; your *girls* could have been killed".

I held up a hand to stop him. "I know, and you're right. But peeping toms at windows are a far step from an assault team in my living room".

"A peeping tom is one thing, Ellie; but one hundred floors up? And underwater?"

Zimmerman briefly looked up from his handheld, where he was processing the data-stream I'd piped out to them. "One hundred twenty-five floors, sir".

"That doesn't make it any better, Ellyandra", Forrest said, turning his attention back to me as he finally sat down, leaned back and rubbed his eyes. "Just think about letting me assign some plain clothes to you – just until we find out who these men worked for".

"I'll think about it, Jim", I answered, sounding more like it was a promise than I'd wanted it to be.

It took me a while to reach my grandfather. Even with silent settings available, he still turned off his communications unit at every play and every movie he went to. Fortunately, I got hold of him before he and the girls headed home, so they didn't have to see all the officers and the entire hubbub. Granddad and I quickly decided that he and the girls would stay the night at a hotel, and he framed it to them like a camping game. After I told each of them I loved them, they were off for an overnight adventure, where they would be safe and sound.

I felt better knowing that my girls and my grandfather were safe, but Forrest was right; it could have been a very different story if they'd been home. I quickstepped around my home as the police officers finished up their work, and Forrest talked to building security. Michaels kept wandering from kitchen to study, passing Zim each time and giving him a number.

"Ok, boys," I said, grabbing a glass of wine from the kitchen and sitting back down on my sofa.

"When are you two going to let me in on what you're doing?"

Zim didn't even look up as he spoke. "Counting footsteps, Ellie".

"Interesting. My home gets invaded, and you two come over to see how many licks it takes to get to the center of a Tootsie Pop?"

Michaels finally stopped, giving Zim one last number. "Fifty-three, with thirty-six inch intervals". With that, Michaels sat down between me and Zim, grabbed my glass of wine, and took a sip.

"The local PD didn't note which of the unconscious men it had removed from what part of your apartment, Ellie. We're noting strides and pathways from what little we can see in the security footage to plot out who moved where while they were in here".

I indignantly took back my wine, asking "OK. Maybe it's late, but that matters why, exactly?"

"If we plot the way they dispersed through your environment, we can try and match it to known military training styles, and see if there is a connection with any known terror groups," Zim answered, still not looking up from his handheld.

"That, and one other thing," Michaels added, reaching for my glass, just as I pulled it away. He stood up, walked into my kitchen, and came back with his own glass of wine, which Zimmerman grabbed as soon as Michaels set it down. "Hey! Get your own glass!" Zim returned the now half-full glass to Michaels, and he finally continued his thought. "There is something about these men, something that rings a bit too familiar, but I just can't place it".

"It's the uniform, Aaron," I answered. "I thought it looked familiar too, but I just can't tell how, or from where".

I could see the wheels spinning in Michael's head, his eyes darting side to side just a bit as he thought. "Uniforms; Hmm." He drank the last of his wine in one gulp, stood up and, turning to leave, said, "Meet me in the holorecreator tomorrow morning. I have an idea".

********

A handful of hours, and more than a few fitful dreams later, I found myself sitting in my office wishing for a caffeine IV. Zimmerman was far too energetic for this time of morning, but despite his eagerness, he gave me time to make a third cup of coffee before we headed to the holorecreator to see what Michaels had come up with. Knowing Michaels, he'd not slept last night; he had likely been up all night, hardly noticing the passage of time as he worked. Of course, that meant he'd crash hard later, but when he was in this zone, I'd learned it was best just to let him run with it.

I had just put the lid on my coffee cup when there was a knock at my office door. Forrest came in and took his usual spot on the opposite side of my desk.

"How is it, Ellyandra," he asked as he sat, "that I am your boss, but I spend more time in your office than you do in mine?"

"Mine's cozy and comfortable; plus, I have a coffee machine". I grabbed a small cup from beside the device my boys had bought for me years ago, and poured up a cup of caffeinated goodness for my boss, handing it to him gently. "What do you have for us, Jim?"

Forrest lifted his handheld and hit the controls with one thumb, scrolling through data like the master he was. "Well, for one thing, there was almost nothing to be found on the men who were taken into custody, but what they did find, I think you'll be interested in".

He hit a few more buttons and the data from his handheld transferred to my desk screen. "OK, so no identification, each had a few papers that were in Cyrillic script? That's odd."

What gets worse is what they did have," Forrest said, gesturing for me to scroll further down.

"One man had a small bag of a white powder, found not to be cocaine, or any other known drug; one of the others was in possession of a metal vial…"

"Sir!" Zim exclaimed on hearing about the vial. "Don't let them open it! It's…"

"Radioactive; yes, they know. They opened that vial in a sealed tank, and it still set off alarms half a building away. Exposure was limited and the officers are being treated".

I scrolled a bit further through the report, and found that aside from radiation exposure medications, the only other thing of note that was found on each of the men was a small metal crucifix, with the Christ figure inverted on the cross.

"Jim," I said quietly. "This weird Crucifix; I've seen it before. We have one just like it with the evidence from the plane crash".

Forrest sat back again, and rubbed the peach-fuzz on the top of his usually bald head as he thought.

"I don't like that connection, Ellie. I don't like it at all".

"So when do we get to interrogate these men?" I asked my boss, realizing that I had just finished my third cup of coffee while reading through the report.

"You don't; the one that cracked his hidden suicide pill in your apartment? Well, they all must have had them. There's no one left *to* interrogate".

That was *not* something I wanted to hear. "OK then, since they died suspiciously in custody, when do I get to *cut them up*?"

Forrest looked at me, shifting uncomfortably in his seat. "Sometimes you enjoy that part of the job just a little too much, Ellyandra". He stood, and added, "I'll have the bodies scanned for your review in the holo morgue. Will that be sufficient?"

I stuck out my lower lip, making the same pouty-face that I'd give the girls when we were play-arguing, and I was losing. "All right, Sir. I guess I can settle for a little holographic catharsis".

# 11

❧

### ❧Illusions❧

Neither Zim nor I knew exactly what Michaels was up to, but neither of us had expected to enter the Holorecreator and see a room full of people. The lights were starting to reflect the power drain as a few more folks appeared here and there, shuffling about and chatting quietly to themselves. Michaels was dashing around, either 'tagging' holograms as possibilities, or deactivating them one by one when they weren't a close match. He barely looked at us when we both walked through a couple of strangers that had just come online. He smiled, looked the new holograms up and down, gave a 'nope, not it' out-loud to the computer, and we watched them both vanish as readily as they had appeared.

"Michaels, where did you find all these people?" I asked, more than a little surprised. "How long have you been at this?"

A sleepy half smile told me he'd been programming this all night. Before he could affirm my theory, Zim piped up, reading from the comm terminal in the holorecreator. "Fifteen hours, and seven hundred twenty-two simulations, Ellie".

Michaels walked over to the Comm and hit a few buttons, and added, "Computer, can you delete the extraneous persons, and convert the shell images to full-holo-scans from existing records?" Zim raised an eyebrow, but didn't say a word. The room started thinning out, and soon only a handful of holo-people surrounded us.

The computer finally answered Michaels query, stating, "Full holo-scan conversion in progress – estimated time to completion, six hours, forty-two minutes".

I walked over to Michaels and placed my hand on his shoulder. "Aaron, you've already been awake all of yesterday, and all last night. We're not twenty anymore". I could see the need for sleep catching up to him more and more each minute. "Care to tell us what you're looking for".

Michaels stretched and yawned like a large feline, every pour of his body exuding exhaustion.

"Uniforms, Ellie". He stood, and started walking Zim and me around the room at the two or so dozen holograms that remained. "All of these outfits look similar to the men who broke into your building last night, but *these* twenty-ish," he said, waving to a group of holograms that looked burned, "they were found in the ruin of the auction house in Miami last fall. And if we can reconstruct the damage, we might be able to make a match".

Last fall, several pirates had fallen when we'd escaped with Erin from the auction place in the Miami Dark Zone; now, here we were again, looking at them for the first time in months. Somehow Aaron was right. As the computer worked to rebuild each detail, they started looking more and more like my intruders.

"Good work Michaels," I said, gesturing for him to sit. "Now, if you don't mind, we're going to do this a little different". Aaron nodded, and I took to the comm to redirect the simulation.

"Computer; identify all current image files from the surface scans, and amalgamate into a single image – clothing only." The room was quickly depopulated as the system built one image from the dozens there had been, then stripped down the human portion to leave only the clothes hanging mid-air.

"Good; now, run simulation MFD-33, but start at time index 20:22, and reverse process the algorithms on the image we just created." It took the computer a few minutes to respond, but the program we'd created for the local fire department was not only found, but reverse applied to the holo-scan of the burned clothing. We sped up the time index, and slowly watched the uniform un-char itself, revealing a military style clothing set that matched the uniforms we had from my now-deceased home invaders.

"Michaels, do you know what this means?" I asked, thinking back to those last hours in the Miami Zone. He nodded slowly.

"Yup; looks like the surviving crew of the MURDERER'S SLAVE decided to pay you a visit".

********

# 12
## ❧Implications❧

"Cheer up, Ellyandra", Director Forrest said, looking over all the data. "It's not everyone who can honestly say they have Pirates after them".

I sat at my desk, pouring over photos from the 'clearing out' of the Miami Dark Zone last fall, looking for faces that matched any of my intruders. I knew that my boss was trying to lighten the mood, but right this moment, light was the last mood I had my mind set on.

"They must've had their second officer take what crew was left, and somehow they made it out of Port in all the mayhem", I said, still scrolling through pics on my comm terminal. "I mean, we knew the sub was gone, so that's not news; but why the hell would they come after me?"

"Revenge? That doesn't match most pirates I've heard about, Ellyandra. The Second Officer is probably glad you fought his boss; meant a promotion for him".

"And why now? Why send resources as scarce as real human beings to come get me here? Wouldn't it make sense to wait till I'm out and about, and easier to grab?"

Forrest nodded as he started skimming more data on the Pirate group. "Looks like we have some intelligence reports from Europe; three months ago, the MURDERER'S SLAVE was reported in Norway, British waters a week before that, then a month later around the Southern Tip of Florida. After that, it fell off the map, so to speak, and no one's seen it since".

As my boss and I tried to make connections to our latest bit of information, Zimmerman came into my office, almost bouncing with excitement. "Ellie, Jim, guess what?"

Director Forrest raised an eyebrow at Zimmerman, and commented quietly to me, "He *never* calls me Jim".

"I've just gotten through with a review of the holo-scans of your attackers; only one of 'em died from a poison cap in his teeth!" Zim hit a few controls on his handheld, and then tapped the corner of my comm, passing the info directly to my terminal. "Looks like the others died of a slow acting poison".

"That sounds more like Pirates, Ellie," Forrest said, tapping his handheld against Zim's to grab the data as well. "If you succeed, you get the antidote; if not, you get the grave".

"Brutal, but oddly effective when trying to control a bunch of criminals". I sat back in my chair, turning this new info over in my head, and glanced over to a picture of my mother, grandfather and my beautiful girls. "Whoever is after me is really serious – too serious for my own comfort".

"You ready for me to assign officers to protect you, Ellyandra?" Jim asked.

"Not me, no sir". I picked up the picture of my family, answering "Though I do have a few people in mind".

********

"Vermont!" Granddaddy shouted. "In April? Are you crazy, child? At my age? It won't be anything close to spring there 'til at least mid-May, or even June!"

I'd known that it wouldn't be a great idea to Granddaddy; as much as he loved Northern New England, his age had finally convinced his body that the cold weather was not his friend.

"Besides, what do you think we'll *do* there? I'll need a hand with the girls, and you *know* there is no way your mother will travel there this time of year!"

I stopped packing the girl's luggage long enough to sit on the bed next to my grandfather. This time last year, he was still in the hospital, dying of asthma, heart trouble, and old age. More than that, he was dying of not living; once he'd made the decision to get up, leave the hospital bed, and live what life he had left, his eyes had lit up like they had when I was child, and despite his grumpiness over the impending trip, I knew that part of him was needing an adventure.

"Don't worry about Mom," I said, putting my arm around his shoulder. "She's in Tanzania, will be for a few months at least. Until then, well, we still have cousins in Vermont and New Hampshire, and they will be helping you. Plus," I paused, reaching into a nearby bag and pulling out a surprise, "I bought you a new camera. You and the girls can take pictures, like you and I used to".

Granddaddy teared up a bit as he took the new camera, and held the sight up to his eyes. "Lens stabilization is good – eyepiece works well with my glasses; fits good in my hands, Ellie. Thank you," he said, reaching over to hug me tight. "You just make damned sure you are here to see all the pictures the girls and I will bring you, got it?" He pushed me back slightly, looked me in the eyes, then took my head in his hands, and kissed my forehead. "Love you, Ellie".

********

A few hours later, my grandfather and my beautiful girls were on a chartered plane, headed to Burlington, Vermont under assumed names, and in the care of FBI professionals trusted with their safety. Olivia had only flown a few times before, but Erin had slept during her flight home from Miami, so she didn't remember the experience. Olivia promised me that *'she and Chester would take good care of Erin and Granddaddy'*, whispering her solemn vow to me as we hugged goodbye.

Forrest, Michaels and Zimmerman stood by me as we watched my heart and souls take off into the hushed night sky. As much as I hated sending them away, I had to admit that it wasn't only for their safety. Now, I could focus, without having to worry. And maybe with a little luck, Charles, my boys and I could create a retroviral for the Porcelain Death before more people died.

********

After a brief round of drinking coffee and finalizing paperwork, I decided that I needed to go see Charles. I would have sooner (let's face it - that kind of argument is not something you can just pretend didn't happen), but the home invasion and realization that I was being hunted had kind of kept me busy. I found myself thinking as I approached his temporary lab in the Federal Building; it was kind of strange that I hadn't heard from him. Even if he didn't want to discuss our argument, keeping quiet about his 'brilliant research' was still not his strongest virtue, and I'd half expected to have him pop up randomly over the last few days just to remind us all how brilliant he was. I knocked on the office door, and heard the hum of machines from inside, but there was no answer, so I knocked again. Still no answer.

"Ok Charlie," I called out. "Don't tell me you cured blindness only to lose your hearing".

Nothing.

I reached out and pushed the handle on the door, letting it slowly open. Light from the hallway poured into the dark room, showing me a well-kept, almost unused looking lab, save for one lone MR-CSA quietly humming away in the corner. I walked in and turned on the overhead lights, only to see that the room had been cleaned of all its work, except for whatever computations he had the MR-CSA working on. I went over to the unit, and pulled its command handheld from the built-in holder on its side. As soon as my fingerprint ID registered, the unit flashed back into scanning mode, verified I really was me, and played a message:

*"Ellie, um... sorry about earlier. I heard over the comm what happened at home, and I know you*

*have your hands full. We need to talk, but... we'll find time later.*

*"In the meantime, I have some equipment at my private lab that looks like it's going to come in handy, so I'm leaving this MR-CSA to finish processing the data on the sample virus we created. It should all be safe - tests show me that it only activates when in a loose, airborne form. Compacted in any container won't allow the virus to become active. Contact me in Van Antwerp if you need me."*

According to the MR-CSA, the message had been recorded the night of the break-in. I hit a few controls to dump the MR-CSA's memory core to the central computer, turned off the lights, and headed down to Old Mobile's Historical and Business District.

*"Hell, the walk will do me good,"* I thought to myself once my shoes hit the old Cobblestone road in front of the Fort Conde Visitors Center. It was only a few blocks to the Van Antwerp building from there, and in short order I found myself standing in front of the first structure in Alabama to have been classified as a 'skyscraper'. In my youth, I'd seen the place crumbling, and the scent of the lobby had an overpowering smell of mildewed wood and motor

oil. Now, a bakery operated at the entryway, filling the lobby with the scent of fresh breads, pastries and other goodies. The entire place simply had a happier feel about it.

The skyscraper had been renovated more times that I could count, and while the interior of the lower levels had been completely modernized, the last round of restoration work above the second floor had kept the look and feel of the building as it had been a hundred years ago. Once I got out of the lift on Charles' floor, the alluring scent of the fresh bread was replaced with something acrid hanging in the air, coupled with occasional whiffs of Ozone. His lab wasn't far from the lift doors, and it was soon evident that the horrible smell was coming from Charles' workspace. The door hung partially opened, and as I drew closer, I had to take part of my shirt and pull it over my nose. *"This looks too familiar"*, I thought to myself, remembering a few years ago when Waldorf's secret police had come gunning for Charlie, and he'd gone into hiding.

I drew my pulser, quietly feeling my way along the wall towards the light switch, then threw the lights on, ready to shoot anything that moved. But there was nothing. In the flickering diode light, I could see the place had been ransacked. Broken comm terminals, beakers and experiments lay shattered either on lab tables, or thrown to the floor. I stepped lightly through the lab, not wanting to disturb any piece of evidence, and thinking, *"I swear to God Charlie, if you've just run off this time, I'm gonna kick your ass"*. Just about then, I saw a hand, laying on the floor, poking out from behind a counter. I nearly tossed my pulser down to run towards Charles, but somehow kept my cool. Forcing down a lump in my throat, I held my breath, and took a few quick steps before I realized that the hand wasn't Charles McFarlane. It couldn't be —it was attached to a porcelain-looking arm that lay severed on the floor.

\*\*\*\*\*\*\*

Zimmerman and Michaels both sat crossed legged on the floor of Charles' lab, as other crime scene analyst from the Mobile PD worked the room. They'd found a small amount of blood smeared near the office door, and there were plenty of signs of a struggle – but because of the porcelain nature of the arm, we couldn't tell who it had come from.

"Looks like it was just broken off Ellie," Zim said, not touching the arm, but using a laser scope to examine the 'wound'. "Yea – pattern look like broken pottery, right through the muscles and bones".

Michaels had a MR-CSA doing a full E-MRI of the arm. "Ellie, I know this sucks to ask, but even going old school, we can't get viable fingerprints off stone, not even with a good E-MRI scan. We sure as hell can't grab any DNA off this. Did Charles have any moles, freckles, birthmarks on his right arm?"

I struggled back in my memory, to images of him I'd tried not to think of for years. Me and Charles at the beach, me and Charles in the pool... me and Charles relaxing as a couple, hardly dressed at all and not caring in the least. I shook my head to refocus my mind.

"No, no birthmarks. No freckles that stand out – just the usual".

"What about tattoos, Ellie?" Zim asked quietly.

I hadn't thought of that in forever. Once, on a trip to Southern Florida, he'd gotten my name tattooed on his wrist. I hadn't gone through with the marking, not because I didn't want to, but because I couldn't deal with the pain. Sure, I had other tats, but nothing on a sensitive area like my wrist. I'd occasionally wondered if he'd had it removed. Thinking about it now, for this reason, put a pit in my stomach, and almost made me ill.

I told the boys about the tattoo, and they projected the E-MRI holo-scan of the arm so we could turn it over and look. There was no tattoo, but that didn't mean he hadn't had the thing removed.

We just had no way to know for sure.

# 13
## ❧Answers☙

"You know he's done this before, Ellyandra" Forrest said, looking over a holo image of Charles' lab. "He'll show up eventually".

I was pacing back and forth in my Boss's office, trying to keep the panic inside me under control. "What about the arm, Jim?" I asked. In my mind's' eye, I could see myself waving the porcelain arm over my head to prove a point. "It didn't just drop out of the sky, so how did it get there? Does it belong to Charles? Or some other poor, one-armed man?"

Forrest dropped the holo image of the lab, and picked up the holo of the arm we'd found, letting it sit in the air in front of him. "There's nothing that says 'who' this came from Ellie," Forrest cajoled. "For all we know, it was an experiment of his while trying to recreate the virus".

"An experiment? Really? I don't remember signing off on a requisition for a *severed human arm*, Jim! Besides, according to his notes…" I paused, shuffling through files on my handheld. I tapped a few controls, displaying a wide variety of notes and specimens to Forrest. "He'd found a way to recreate the viral structure using a different technique that revolved around a different radiation signature. Last thing I see here is that he was working on an inject-able form".

"I'll admit, it's all damn peculiar". Forrest leaned back in his chair, and let out a deep sigh. "But he's damned peculiar anyway. I've put a watch out for his credentials to be flagged if anyone uses them. If someone has him, they took him for a reason; and they try to get into any secured areas based off his temporary creds, we will know. And if *he* tries to use those credentials anywhere, we'll know. All we have to do is wait, and listen".

I wasn't about to argue with my boss. The man had stood at my side and backed me up more times than I could count, and bosses like those don't come along every day. I half-heartedly agreed with him, and headed back to the cubicle farm where Zim and Michaels were set up. I was upset and worried to the point where I didn't even want coffee, but I hoped my boys may have some ideas that my clouded mind was missing.

********

I usually LOVE long weekends, but not this time. Of course, it wasn't really a long weekend. This time, there were no extra days off to look forward to. It was long because I spent it waiting; waiting to hear from my girls (who were having a fantastic time trudging about in the remaining snows of Vermont); waiting for additional testing on the arm I found in the lab; waiting for any word from a man I once loved, and despite his arrogance and pretentiousness, still found myself caring about as a dear friend.

Some people may not understand the dichotomy that comes with both caring about someone, and wanting to strangle them senseless at the same time. I definitely had wanted to strangle Charles more often than I'd care to admit. We'd been as close as people can get, and been driven apart with as much animosity as one can imagine. We'd spent years both hating and loving each other, and now, with his uncharacteristically emotional reasons finally revealed, I felt like our friendship might finally be able to be a strong, truthful, and stable one. And honestly, *that* is a concept I'd never fully had with him before, even while we were engaged.

*"And then he up and vanishes – again",* I said to myself, puttering around my home and trying to stay busy. *"I swear to God he'd better be missing an arm when we find him".*

\*\*\*\*\*\*\*\*

Monday finally arrived, but this time it was without its usual level of disdain. I was in the office early, ready and waiting for my boys to come in, so we could tackle the virus, and our missing scientist together. I spent my morning poring over reports from the weekend; no new victims of the *Porcelain Death* had been found, and no one-armed men had been treated at any of the area hospitals. By the time Michaels and Zimmerman arrived, I found that was the only bit of information we'd gathered over the weekend. There had been no hits on the use of Charles' Federal Credentials.

It was around noon when Zim, who'd been setting up additional equipment to monitor for *any* communication from Charles, nearly leapt into my office with a shout.

"Ellie! We've got him!"

Before I could even get a question out of my mouth, he'd hopped away excitedly, quickly jumping back to his cubicle, which I found was now stuffed with old radio equipment in addition to his usual assortment of technology both old and new.

"What do you have, Zim?" I asked as I settled into a small available space between the piled-up radio equipment and a few old PC's that were stacked one on top of the other.

Zimmerman reached up to an old-style box speaker that he'd cross wired into the radio system, and turned up the volume.

"Clicking. You called me over here for clicking", I responded coolly, trying to keep my irritation in check. "Odd, I've never heard Charlie click before".

Just then, Michaels rounded the corner, and placed a small microphone up to the speaker, which Zim plugged into his main comm. The computer immediately started translating the clicks into a modified Morse code, which it then translated:

iMduxYrXr8E1y4Blpy5K
iMduxYrXr8E1y4Blpy5K
iMduxYrXr8E1y4Blpy5K

"What is that Zim?" I asked, surprised enough by the fact that either Zim or Michaels had recognized Morse code from the quiet series of clicks they'd shown me.

"That's the Ident code tied to Charles McFarlane's Federal ID Badge".

\*\*\*\*\*\*\*\*

The next few hours were a blur. Forrest had to call in more than a couple of favors to FBI offices spread across the country, finding not only old radio equipment that still worked, but anyone who knew enough about it to follow Zim's instructions on setting up a net to triangulate the signals' origin. Oddly, the credentials hadn't been used, the code was just being transmitted, which was a damned strange way for us to find him. By Five PM, we had twelve facilities in ten states, and within another hour, we'd been able to find the source of the signal.

Somehow, for some reason, Charles (or his ID Badge at least) was in Nevada. As soon as we pinpointed the location of the signal, and cross referenced it with a map of Government facilities, it was quickly evident why.

The signal originated a scant ten miles outside of the Yucca Mountain Nuclear Waste Repository.

14
~Sightings~

Late night flights and rough mountain roads are some of my least favorite things, and on this trip, I had them both in multitudes. Even with modern air travel being faster and safer than it had been when I was little, it still sucked having to catch multiple flights in the middle of the night. Plus, sleeping on a plane was never my strong point anyway. A few late night layovers, changing of flights and finally getting to Las Vegas, Nevada was nothing compared to grabbing our gear and stuffing it (and ourselves) into the compact, non-computer driven All-Terrain Vehicle that was waiting for us. Plus, if anyone ever tells you that the desert is hot, ask them to define *at what time* they are talking about; it was, as my Aunt Michelle would have said, as *'cold as a witches' tit in a brass bra in the middle of January'* when we got off that last plane. We landed at four in the morning, had to pack our crap (at this hour anything that wasn't my bed or my kids qualified as 'crap') while we were freezing and half asleep, and on top of that, we had at least a two-hour drive in front of us before we could even get close to Yucca Mountain. It would probably take longer, since the roads to the now defunct facility had been closed for fifteen years.

Cranky? Yeah, maybe just a little.

Not being able to sleep gave me a few 'quiet' moments to meditate a little, gather my thoughts, and look over the last of the notes we'd recovered from Charles' lab. He'd done several dozen searches on radioactive materials in the Federal Database, and kept looking for a specific combination of available isotopes in whatever form he could find them. Since Yucca Mountain had been shut down for so long, it took him a while to reach those results, but apparently he hit the jackpot searching its inventory. There were no further searches afterwards.

It was seven forty-five when we hit the perimeter fence around the entrance to Yucca Mountain. I'd gotten a lot of research done, though I must admit that I had dozed off a bit here and there, so some of my information felt like something I'd seen in dreams. And if I was honest with myself, I wasn't sure if I could tell the difference between what I'd read, and what I'd imagined.

"Aaron," I said quietly in the morning light. "The main fence is opened. We should be seeing a gate soon, shouldn't we?" I asked, already knowing the protocol said that we should have seen a gate a mile back.

"Yeah, Ellie. You're right. That's... not standard procedure". He slowed the vehicle enough so he could safely turn around and jab Zimmerman in the ribs. Zim had zonked out almost as soon as we left Vegas, and despite the bad roads, had been peacefully snoozing for the entire trip. If any of us was really rested, it was Zim.

"What?! Wha... HEY!" Zim stammered as his brain reconnected not only with his body, but the real world. "That hurt!"

"Woke you up, didn't it?" Michaels responded, interrupting Zim's protest with, "Don't start with me kid. Last time I had to wake you up, it took me a damned hour, and we don't have that kind of time".

Zim looked a little sheepish as he let out one last yawn, and added, "Sun's up. We'll need to act as fast as we can so the heat doesn't catch us. We only have a couple liters of water".

"Maybe, maybe not," Michaels answered, hitting the pedal just enough to unsettle both me and Zimmerman. "We're at a high elevation, so we're not likely to find scorching temps or tumbleweeds. Let's find that guard post; gotta be along this road somewhere".

It only took a mile, maybe a mile and a half, before we saw another fence, and *this time*, we found the expected guard post. After we'd crossed the initial perimeter, we'd seen sign after sign warning us that this was an unsafe area, a government controlled area, a radiation risk, etc...etc...etc... exactly what we'd expected to see. But the closer we got to the guard post, the more its stoic silence gave me a sense of dread.

"Aaron," I said, almost whispering, even though I didn't have any reason to. "Slow down, and pull up off the road, alongside the guard post".

"They won't like that, Ellie", he said in protest, but a quick glance from me told him that I didn't give a damn what they liked, so Michaels pulled off the road slowly, and parked our vehicle just off to one side of the guard's shelter.

No one came out. We were met with a small breeze that blew around dust and debris, and a silence you could feel as it lay on your shoulders.

I grabbed my pulser from her charging port in the vehicle, and put my hand on the door latch. Seeing this, Aaron turned off the transport, and both he and Zim armed themselves as well; we all stepped out of the vehicle into the dirt and dust around us.

Even though it wasn't quite eight o'clock, there was a haze in the air that made it hard to see exactly where the sun was. The building dust-storm wasn't any help either, but we'd been warned of the possibility, so my team and I all pulled our ample turtleneck collars out from under our garb, and used them to mask our noses as best as we could from the dust. Our 'wind-shades' that had been given to us with our gear in Vegas wrapped around our ears and our eyes, so we were as best protected as we could be given the situation.

Michaels started to approach the guard post, but I gently grabbed his arm and shook my head no. I gave him a signal to stay back, and he stepped aside so I could enter first.

The space was exactly as you would expect it to be; very small, no frills, barely sealed off from the elements by a thin acrylic pane and a nearly useless door. There was a comm unit, a small desk, a *tiny* toilet in one corner, and the main control for the gate. I got the impression that serving 'gate duty' was a worse punishment than peeling potatoes, since this was isolated, cramped, nasty, and mostly pointless.

As much as the state of the place disgusted me, it really wasn't surprising to see that a corpse was sitting at the desk. I tried to wave Zim and Michaels into the tiny room, but there almost wasn't room for three of us (or four, depending on how you counted), so they stood in the doorway as I moved toward the body. The emblems on the uniform clearly identified this person as an MP (Military Police). As soon as I touched the corpse, I knew we had another victim.

"Zim, Aaron," I started, pausing to get my breath. "He's stone".

********

It took me and my boys a good ten minutes to remove the body from where it was seated. Unlike our previous victims, this person seemed to have succumbed to the *Porcelain Death* quickly, and what was left was like a grotesque sculpture made of a man in his death throws. The face was twisted in obvious pain, and the fingers had been almost buried in the wooden desk, most breaking off as we moved the body. This victim also seemed to be more brittle than the ones we'd run across before, falling apart as we tried to move him.

While Michaels and I worked with the MP in the guard station, I sent Zim to scout into the main development and see what he could find out. Normally, Zim *loved* playing recon; it brought out the little kid in him (if that little kid had seven doctorates in Computer Sciences, spoke Klingon, and still went 'pew pew' when firing his pulser). This time, though, I don't think he enjoyed himself. It only took ten minutes for him to return, with a duffle bag of items across his back, and a grim look on his face.

"What did you find?" I asked, reaching for the sack.

"More of … more of *this*", he answered, gesturing toward the MP we had been examining.

"Everyone looks like they were fighting it; not like the plane victims at all".

"Or like the man in Bienville Square", Michaels added.

"But what does that give us?" I demanded. Neither of my boys could answer, so I kept pressing. "So none of the victims we've seen so far have looked like... like 'this'; what is the difference?"

Michaels bent down to look at the body of the MP again. Zimmerman looked away towards the sky, deep in thought.

Me? I waited; I knew I didn't have the answer outright. I also knew that between the three of us, we had more brainpower in this small space than most people would have in a full office. We were used to thinking 'outside the box', so I sat, I thought, and I waited to see what my boys would offer.

After a few minutes, I looked at each member of my team. Michaels was still studying the MP closely, but just looking at him, I could see that each additional sweep of the body was giving him nothing new. He'd been done after his first pass, not due to negligence, but due to talent. I left him to keep looking, and moved my gaze to Zim.

Zim was still looking out of the acrylic window into the hazy sky around us, his eyes unfocused and purposely empty. As soon as I saw his face, I saw *where* he was; I remembered this look, even though I hadn't seen it in a few years on his face.

"Zim," I offered softly. "I've seen those eyes in your head before. I know it hurts, but", I paused and looked at Michaels, who'd turned his attention to the two of us; "WE need you to tell us what you are thinking. You've seen this before, am I right?"

"Not this exactly, El; something pretty close, but not this". Zimmerman lowered his head from the sky, but he couldn't hide the small tears that had begun to stream from his eyes, as much as he might want to. "It's... it's nothing; just a bad memory".

"Shiloh Yemini Zimmerman!" I exclaimed, grabbing Zim by the shoulders and *making* him look me in the eyes. "I know that look; you've seen this before; bad memory or not, you *need* to tell me anything you can. That is your job, and that is what you *PROMISED ME* when you came back to Mobile".

Zim shook his head a bit, but didn't try to break away at all. "Zim," I added quietly, "I'm not just asking for me; I'm asking for *you* too".

It took a moment, but Zim finally nodded in approval, and moved out of my loose clasp to sit on the small desk in the guard post.

"Bev…" he paused, as though the feel of the name on his tongue caused him pain. "Beverly died in the Zone in St. Louis; you know that".

Michaels and I both quietly nodded. Zim had **never** talked to us about St. Louis, not in the two plus years since the incident happened, and he'd come home to Mobile.

"I've seen that look, Ellie," Zim offered, holding himself up as best as he could. As much as he fought to look OK, I knew better, and could easily see the pain this was putting him through, but neither Michaels nor I stopped him. This had been a long time coming, and finally, Zim had hit something in the field that was making him face these memories.

"They gunned her down, right there in the street. I tried to pull her away, but she *kept fighting back,* kept firing the pulser she had, kept grabbing hold of... of me, like I could help her; like, if she didn't let go of *me*, she could take any bullet, and still keep fighting".

Tears were streaking down Zimmerman's cheeks now, but I knew that if I reached out first, it would shut him down. As much as we needed to know what insight he could offer here and now, Zim needed to finally get this out. It had been buried, growing, festering, for far too long. And if he didn't face it, the memories would eventually kill him. So timing be damned, here we were, listening, and waiting.

"Did they tell you when I ran, Ellie?" Zim asked through his tears. "Did they tell you that I was *holding her* in my arms, firing back with a gun we'd picked up, because the pulsers were dead? Did they tell you that she was so shot up that she fell apart in my arms?" Zimmerman stood up, anger and pain in his face, and looked down to me, almost screaming, "DID THEY EVER TELL YOU?"

I didn't flinch; not one muscle. Point One: I knew that as hurt as he was, *my* Shiloh Zimmerman would never hurt me. And even if he did, he wouldn't mean it. When you love someone, as I loved my boys – you forgive. It is as simple as that. And if you don't forgive, well, you never loved them the way you thought you did.

With that in mind: Point Two: my friend, who was hurting, had asked me a question. And he deserved an answer.

"Zim, no one ever told me the details. They wanted to wait until *you* could tell me".

Almost immediately, the hurt and anger in Zim's face relaxed, leaving behind a very tired looking man who'd been hiding his pain for years. I knew he was always there, in between the moments of forced normalcy and desperate attempts to reconcile what he'd seen as his failure. And what he'd missed, even after all this time, is that the love of his life, *his* Beverly, had died not only doing and fighting for what she believed in, but she did it at the side of a man she loved and trusted with more than her life.

After the events of the last few weeks, plugging in Zim's experience with my own seemed almost too easy, despite the years of regret Charles and I had. I reached towards him, and took Zim's chin in my small hand, gently raising it until he could look me in the eye.

"Hon, after the crap I've been through with Charlie over the last month, I think I understand you more now than I ever have". Zim started to speak, but I placed a finger across his lips, and added, "No words, my dear. Not on this. You are going to be fine, and you know I've got you; I've *always* got you. But you came here with me for a reason. I 'need' to know… what connection are you seeing, Shiloh?"

I made sure when I used his given name that I mimicked the same inflection I'd heard his mother use a few years before. I had no interest in 'tricking' my suffering friend, but if I could offer him any degree of comfort, and still fulfill our reason for being here, I wanted to do so.

Zim gently took my hand away from his face, and slowly stood. He moved purposefully across the small space toward the corpse of the MP, and gently, almost tenderly, drew his hand across the face of the deceased man, trying futilely to close the eyes that were now set in stone.

"She had this…look. Before I ran; before she started coming apart and falling into pieces; before the recovery drones burned her away. Her face was locked – just like this. This expression, the pain, the...

she was FIGHTING for her LIFE! *THIS* was her... her face… when... she..."

"When she died, Zim," Aaron answered, gently putting his arm around Zimmerman's shoulder, and moving him cautiously away from the body of the MP. "Kara had the same look, even though I didn't see her body until weeks after; that look was there, it was 'stuck' there, right?" Zimmerman nodded a little, and then Michaels added, "It just doesn't fit them, does it?"

In all the years I'd known Aaron Michaels since his wife and baby daughters had been brutally murdered, this was the only time I could think of when he had used his wife's name. He'd spoken of her, in passing, but it was always 'his wife', and 'his daughter'; saying her name had become something sacred to Aaron. Zim had looked a little puzzled at first, but being as brilliant as he was, he quickly made the connection, and he and Michaels sat close to each other in a bond of friendship and murdered loves. I knew I didn't have a place in that embrace, and I hoped, as much as I loved them both, to avoid a membership in that club.

While my boys commiserated, I decided to go through the duffle of items Zimmerman had brought back from his recon. There were a few 'hard items' on top; things like security keys and a couple of high-powered holographic portables. That would have been great if we had computer access here. We could have basically *made* anything we needed, short of food and toilet paper. But without command codes, we'd been left in a lurch. I could only hope that between the junk Zimmerman had retrieved, and the radiation suites he'd packed at the bottom of the bag, that we stood a fighting chance of finding what we were here to find.

\*\*\*\*\*\*

## 15
### ～Graveyard∾

I gave Michaels and Zimmerman as much time as they needed. If they had been 'normal' in any way, we'd have been dead in the water. But, knowing my boys, and the unusual way they were put together, I wasn't surprised when they both suited up in the radiation gear a half hour later, ready to tackle whatever lay ahead of us.

Donning the protection gear reminded me of just how little had changed sometimes. I remembered watching old movies with my grandfather when I was really small, and the radiation suits in classic sci-fi looked almost exactly like what we were wearing now, right down to the hideous bright-yellow colour.

At least we didn't have to put on the helmets until we actually went into the storage facility, so for the moment, we could breathe easily.

The main entrance to Yucca Mountain was only a short distance away from the guard post, so we walked, leaving our transport where we'd parked it. Back before the Greater Depression, the government had started on this place, literally digging a giant tunnel into the mountainside. One of the giant tunneling machines still sat off to the left of the main entrance, rusted and broken. Over the years, the place had been closed, reopened, closed again, added onto, and changed up at least a dozen times. Large pipes crawled across the face of the mountain and into the tunnel, and still left room for multiple vehicles to come and go through at the same time. Once we had passed through the enormous main entrance, and were in the shadow of the mountain, the air around us started to cool.

"Well, the power is still on," Michaels observed, noting the overhead lighting that filled the area. "But where is everyone?"

We both looked to Zim. "The group I found was down the main corridor, just in front of the elevators. Seven people, at least; maybe a few more".

"Let's start over there," I gestured to the right, pointing out a structure that looked like it had been built into the side of the tunnel. "According to the intel report, that should be a shipment supervisor's office. Let's start there".

The office had several windows that opened into the large receiving area, and the lights inside the office were off. Opening the door, we hit the light switch only to discover that the room had been used as a dumping ground for the dead. At least a dozen men and women in US Army uniforms had been piled up in this room. They had obviously been tossed haphazardly in, one on top of another. Each one had a pained and horrified look frozen on their glazed, porcelain faces.

********

Initially, we thought we'd give a quick once-over on the victims we found in Yucca Mountain, but as we made our way towards the actual storage areas, we found more and more of the dead. By the time we reached the main elevators that would take us to the underground storage, we'd already counted ten more bodies, each showing the tell-tale porcelain looking skin, and each one showing a look of pure agony on their faces that were now locked in an eternal, almost ceramic work of macabre sculpture.

"Do you have any idea where we are going, Ellie?" Michaels asked, manually opening the lift doors for us.

"I was reading Charlie's notes from the MR-CSA he'd left running" I answered as we all entered the lift. "Looks like what he specifically needed was on Level 62, Section C.

"Hope you're not out of shape Zim," Michaels quipped as he closed the lift doors. "This thing only goes down to Level 50". The elevator started moving, and we could see the lights from each floor shining from under the doorways as we passed by. "I just hope we can find the stairs".

"I just hope we find Charles McFarlane", I added quietly, getting small nods from each of them.

The trip down to Level 50 took a good five minutes, and I could feel the pressure changing in my ears as we went further under the mountain. When the lift doors opened, we entered the hallway to discover that the red, spinning Emergency Lights had been activated. The turning hazard lights made the scene look more like a late-night traffic stop than a hallway, and the low lights spinning round and round cast moving shadows on the walls.

I took out my handheld, switching on its high-powered light to scan the dark walls. Soon, I found the evacuation plan on the across from the elevator entrance, and quickly started planning our route to the stairs that led down.

"We've got to go thru Section A on this level, and around past some storage racks to get to the stairwell". I put on the protective headgear that went with the radiation suit, and, using my handheld as a flashlight, we turned out of the hallway and went down the corridor towards Section A.

About fifty feet down the main hall, we found the entrance to Section A. Once inside, we found the same red spinning hazard lights, and still no further signs of people. The room was huge, and filled with row upon row of metal storage racks that went from floor to ceiling. Each shelf had some kind of container on it, everything from oil drums and wooden crates to large, ceramic urns, and every item was literally strapped down to its shelf, and labeled with a code and info sheet showing its contents. Aside from our own breathing and footsteps, there wasn't a single sound. It was actually so quiet, that the silence almost hurt my ears as they futilely strained to catch any inkling of life around us.

The door to the stairwell was propped open, but no emergency lights were on either up or down the passageways' concrete walls. It was so dark that actually closing your eyes almost made the place seem brighter. While I knew my mind was playing tricks, it even seemed like the light from my handheld didn't cast itself as far as it had earlier, and I knew that if we lost our lights in this stairwell, we'd be fighting both fear and darkness to get to level 62.

One or two levels of stairs is no problem, even in the dark. But twelve of them is taxing on both the legs and the nerves. When we reached the bottom, the radiation meters on our handhelds were quietly clicking away like mad, and when we opened the door to the main hallway, the sound was almost like thunder rumbling wildly through the almost endless silence. The floor was littered with dark, shadowy objects of various sizes, strewn all about the area. Once I took my handheld to examine the object, I realized what they were.

"Boys, these were people". I swung my light around at different pieces of people who'd been killed by the *Porcelain Death*, then literally shattered into pieces. With our lights, you could easily see a hand, an arm, part of a face; whoever did this was both sick and brutal.

"Come on boys; there's nothing we can do here". I stood up and walked around the ocean of racks and storage looking for labels or directions through this dark maze. Eventually, we found another hallway, and a set of steel and lead-lined doors that were marked 'SECTION C'. The door was left slightly opened.

********

Once we were inside, we made a sweep of the room. I had Michaels go around the walls, and Zim and I split up the rows of racks until we'd met in the middle. There was low overhead lighting, casting shadows of impenetrable darkness here and there, and a couple of the spinning emergency lights were still running above the doorway. On the back wall of this area was a rickety cargo elevator, but the control panel for it had been ripped apart. Michaels stepped near the broken controls, and took off his headgear just long enough to sniff the wires.

"This was recent, Ellie," he said, placing the protective, windowed headpiece back on. "Want me to fix it?"

Before I could answer, Zim chimed in. "My legs want you to fix it, Aaron. I can't do those stairs again!"

Michaels turned back to the control panel with a laugh. "Well, whoever tore this thing apart did more cosmetic damage than actual wiring damage. This isn't so bad; not impossible at all".

It didn't take us long to find the spots that had held whatever items or substances had interested Charlie. There were a handful of shelves where the straps had been cut, and the storage items and their data sheets had been removed. The radiation meters in my handheld were going wild now, and I had a feeling that whatever protective protocols had been in place for these items, something had gone horribly wrong, seals had been broken, and without these suits, we'd all be in big trouble.

"Ellie," Zim said from the other side of the room. "Come here, please. You need to see this".

I went around three aisles to find Zim standing with his handheld pointing its light towards the floor. There was broken glass, some sort of yellowish, gooey substance, and torn fabric that was the same awful colour as our radiation suits. I quickly swung my light around and noticed more torn suit pieces stuck here and there on jagged edges of racks and containers, and even a smear of blood on one supporting steel beam.

"Someone put up one hell of a fight," I said, grabbing a blood sample with the tiny testing arm of my handheld. "With the piss poor signal strength we're getting here, it'll take us at least an hour to see who this belongs to".

I set my handheld to connect and process the info as soon as we had a signal, and continued surveying the area. The room was somewhere around 10,000 square feet, but the passageways between the storage racks were snug, and two people couldn't have passed each other easily in the narrow rows. At the end of row 15, I found a comm terminal.

"Zim," I asked, "Do you still have those ID cards you found earlier? Didn't they have a swipe strip?"

Zim came up from the other side of the row, shuffling through the duffle bag he'd brought, and handed me a couple if ID cards. I hit the main power button on the interface panel, and the comm came up to a password prompt. The first card returned an ACCESS DENIED error, and a single asterisks appeared in red in the upper right hand corner of the black screen.

"Ok; that one didn't cut it. Let's try... this one", I said, tossing the first card aside and grabbing another from the small stack. Again, I got ACCESS DENIED, and a second red asterisks appeared beside the first; the two of them were flashing now.

"Why do I get the feeling I've only got one more shot at this, Zim?" I asked as I took one of the two remaining ID cards from him. "Here goes nothing" I said as I slid the card through the scanner.

WELCOME, DR. RICHARDS.
1) General Communications
2) New Inventory
3) Old Inventory
4) Section C Security

"Jackpot!" I exclaimed, clapping my gloved hands together. Now, the question is, where do we go from here?

Zimmerman stepped up to me, and gently motioned towards the terminal. "Don't worry about that Ellie. I've got this," he said, smiling broadly.

I'm not sure what combination of keystrokes and functions Zim put into that comm terminal, but in just a few side-screens, we could see the entire directory for the facility. I almost jumped out of my skin when I saw that the security cameras fed directly into this system. Someone had beat us here, and damn it this could at least tell us more about what happened. I took my handheld, and tapped the corner of the comm terminal to download the data. Between the blood analysis and all the recording of info I'd done since leaving Mobile, I was starting to push the limits of the handheld, especially since we were off the grid and couldn't hit the cloud for more processing power or storage. I grabbed the security footage for the last few days, and Zim grabbed the Section C inventory, so he could compare the numbers against the empty spaces and find out what was taken.

It was just about then that we heard something on the floors above us. This deep, echoing noise, as though a jeep had been dropped down a mine shaft, rattled through the entire mountain. It was loud enough to wake the dead, if the dead around here had been merely sleeping. Zim and I looked to Michaels, who picked up the pace of his work on the elevator controls. I went back into the hallway, running as best as I could in the darkness toward the stairwell. The door was shut, and locked from the other side.

"Damn! We're trapped here if you can't fix that lift, Michaels!" I said, running back to the storage room.

"I've just about – GOT IT!" Michaels cried, as sparks flew from the broken control panel, and the elevator above started its slow decent toward us. Another loud, booming sound startled us, shaking dust and dirt from the ceiling above.

"That was an explosion, Ellie. Sounds like someone is trying to bury us here".

"Can't the damn thing go any faster?" I asked, pushing the now-connected call button repeatedly.

Two more explosions rocked the facility above us before the elevator finally reached us. As the cargo lift started its crawl back to the surface, we could see damaged areas on the other side of the grate that separated the car and its contents from the floors as we passed by. Another BOOM rocked the facility, and floors started to cave in. We just reached the top of the lift shaft when the last of the explosions rocked the ground around us, and we literally had to crawl our way through the rubble outside the secondary entrance we'd been delivered to.

It took us a moment to pull ourselves together, and get out of the protective gear now that we didn't need it. The entryway we'd pulled ourselves out of was off to the right of the main entrance. There was still a lot of rumbling from the ground beneath us as Yucca Mountain collapsed in on itself, but for the moment, we seemed to be safe.

"Everyone alright?" I asked, lending Zim a hand to help him to his feet. My boys nodded, tossing aside the radiation suits, "Ok, then. Let's get back to the transport and get the hell out of here. We'll call Forrest and have him send a team in to investigate this". Headed back to the guard post, we rounded the corner towards the main entrance just in time to see a jeep being loaded with men, one of which was handcuffed, and looked wounded. He was wearing a torn radiation suit.

"CHARLES!" I screamed. He looked up and around, and just for a second, we locked eyes. But what I saw in his eyes wasn't happiness, or relief that we were here. All I saw was fear and sadness.

One of the other men close to him hit Charles over the head, and tossed him in the back of the jeep like garbage. Another jumped into the driver's seat, while three others started firing automatic rifles at us. My boys and I pulled our pulsers and reciprocated with not only electric shots, but sound waves that were strong enough to bring down a Rhino. We ran towards them, firing over and over, and trying to make it to our vehicle. One of Aaron's shots tagged a man standing in the back of the jeep, and he fell out onto the ground head first as they pulled away. They didn't slow or stop, but kept driving, easily outpacing us and escaping.

I stopped by the body of the fallen man, expecting to find him to be tricked out in pretend military garb. So many private armed groups wanted to play soldier these days, that you always expected that, but this guy, aside from the rifle he'd taken with him in his fall, and a brown poncho, he wasn't military at all; plain jeans and a white T-shirt, with a Hawaiian shirt over that. No extra clips of bullets, no boot knives (or even boots; he was wearing dock shoes), no grenades or anything else that screamed soldier. The fall had snapped his neck when he hit the ground, so we'd never be able to really ask him what he was doing here. I went to turn the body over for examination as Michaels came up behind me.

"Our transport is dead, Ellie. They slashed all four tires. We're not going anywhere".

Zim stepped up, saying, "No worries. Now that we aren't so far underground, I've got a signal on my handheld. I'll contact Forrest and have him send help.

I nodded in approval as I finished turning the body, when something fell out of the victim's top pocket. All three of us went silent when I picked up another one of the odd looking Crucifixes.

"Gentlemen. I think we are dealing with a cult".

# 16
## ❧Dogma❧

Forrest sent a helicopter to pick us up, and I spent the hour long ride back crammed in the backseat of the tiny cockpit, sitting next to a body bag containing our dead assailant. I won't go into the details about the level of pure discomfort, and I certainly won't talk about the smell. Let's just say that I've had better ways of spending an hour.

The FBI office in Vegas was extremely generous with their resources when they found out what had happened at Yucca Mountain. While the place had been a pariah politically, in truth people had just been afraid that someone would blow it up, and irradiate the entire State. Now that someone *had* blown it up, and the mountain had responded by further burying all the dangerous material as it had been designed to do, people were pissed that an *'important source of jobs and revenue for the State of Nevada"* had been destroyed.

As much as hypocritical people bothered me, the creepy crucifix in my hand was starting to bother me more. Ever since we'd seen the first one from the pockets of Passenger 303, it had stayed in the back of my mind. Funny thing was, it wasn't an inverted crucifix; the Jesus on it was right side up, if you looked at the tiny writing, the INRI, over his head, you could easily see the direction of the letters, and determine top and bottom. The cross itself was what was reversed, and His body position changed accordingly. And while I'd heard of people being crucified upside-down (such as the crucifixion of St. Peter), in this case, it was only the cross that was inverted, placing the body in an unnatural splayed position. As much as I had always enjoyed the psychological aspects of studying world religions, I didn't have anywhere near the Theological expertise to even begin to tackle the meaning.

While the folks in Las Vegas were very giving, they pretty much left us alone. Unlike my time spent last year in Miami, where the local supervisors and agents were always underfoot, these guys basically handed us keys and pass-codes, and said 'have at it, friend,' while they went about their own business. Honestly, I was kind of glad.

Forrest had brought the E-MRI scans and holo image records of both Passenger 303, and the first victim we'd found in Bienville Square, so we could get another look at both of them. We'd planned on flying back to Mobile in the morning, but now that I knew Charles was not only alive, but had *both* of his arms and looked relatively uninjured, I didn't plan on heading home until I had something that was helping me find my friend. On top of that, I had a feeling that whatever had been taken from Yucca Mountain was far more dangerous in the hands of Charles' captors, so we really needed to find both Charles McFarlane, and the dangerous materials that were likely with him.

"Jim," I asked as we passed in the hallway. "Isn't there a National Database for religious Cults operating in America?"

My boss stopped, and rubbed his fuzzy head, letting out a long, slow breath. "Well, Ellie, there was a while back. But after the United Inter-Faith Initiative and its First Amendment case against the

NSA a few years ago, I'm pretty sure it was shut down".

I looked Jim in the eyes. I'd seen this deviousness before.

"So I should ask Zim to find it and hack it. Got it," I said joyfully, turning to skip away down the hall.

********

While Zimmerman was busy doing that side project for me, Michaels and I set up the local holo-morgue to process the data from Passenger 303 first. After an hour, the image processors were ready, and good old 303 appeared in front of us.

We poured over 303 for another hour, peeling back layers of digital skin, muscle and going all the way down to the bones. Once we had 303 peeled back as far as we could, we set the computer to literally scan his bone structure for tiny computer chips, wiring, or radiation damage to the calcium lattice that made the bones what they were. We found exactly what we'd found before; no tiny computer chips, no hidden electrodes, and radiation damage at the end of the bone where his leg had been severed surgically to make room for the prosthesis.

As much as we hated to admit it, 303 was a dead end. Whoever was orchestrating this had done a *very* thorough job in covering their tracks. We decided we'd put away Passenger 303 for now, and started loading our vagabond, Preston Woodridge, into the holo system.

It would take the system a while to build the holographic image, so Michaels and I hopped down to the local sub shop to grab some sandwiches for all of us. Twenty minutes and seventy-five credits later, we strolled back into the office, dropping off a pastrami and cheese foot-long to Director Forrest, and taking a Brisket sandwich with Red Cabbage and smoked cheese to Zim, which he devoured in five bites without even looking up from his keyboard. Not wanting to interrupt him, we started to walk away, but Zim stopped us by quietly saying two things.

"Thanks for the sandwich. I found the site you were looking for"

I placed my hand gently on Zim's shoulder, looking at his screen. "Zim, hon; that's the dark web".

"Where else do you think the Government would hide it after it was deemed illegal?"

The webpage header clearly advertised what this site was. And after Zim checked and double checked not only the metadata, but hacked the directory to actually *see* the files that made up the site, we confirmed that this was either the best, most detail-oriented forgery we'd ever seen, or this was indeed what had become of the 'United States Government Index of American Religious Activity: Offshoots, Cults and Other Terrorist Organizations" website.

"Is it still searchable, Zim?" I asked, pulling up a seat and finishing the last bites of my own lunch.

"Looks like it, Ellie. What do I search for?"

Michaels' alarm went off, telling us that our new holo image was ready for review. "El, he's ready. Mind if we come back?"

"Sure thing," I answered, standing back up and putting my chair back. "Zim, search for inverted or unusual crosses, specifically Crucifixes. Let's see if this creepy thing is linked to any particular group, and we can go from there".

Zim nodded, taking the drink we'd brought him and nearly inhaling half of it in one long slurp.

Michaels and I went back to the holo morgue, and saw that Preston Woodridge, our first victim from Bienville Square, was ready and waiting for us.

"Ellie?" Michaels inquired. "Didn't his sister live in Mobile? I don't remember what happened when you talked to her".

"I never got to talk to her Aaron. When I found the address, no one there even...damn!"

"Damn what, Ellie?" Michaels moved closer to me, and asked excitedly, "Come on! What?"

"The people there said she'd gone off to live at some church. Damn it! How could I forget that, Aaron?"

Michaels was quiet for a moment. Then, he simply said, "El, you're human. You remembered it now. Don't sweat it".

I took a deep breath, let it slowly out, then nodded to the holographic body before us. "Alright, then let's take a look here, and see what we can see".

We started with this victim just as we had with 303; *'computer, take away clothing, but leave any contents of pockets for review'; computer, remove all excess material from the pockets; computer scan the body for any scars, incisions or technology, and display above the body as an independent image'*. One change after another gave us nothing new. Finally, a good fifty minutes in, I gave the command, *'computer, peel away the skin, past the epidermis and dermis, down to the muscle; remove extraneous fat as well'*.

This one seemed to take the computer a bit longer to process, but after a good two minutes of beeps, whirs and general boredom, the skin of

Preston Woodridge vanished, leaving behind a gruesome, muscle-covered skeleton.

"It always reminds me of the Mutter Museum," Aaron commented, remembering the traveling exhibit we'd both seen as teenagers.

"We'd never have seen it as kids if they hadn't brought part of it to Mobile," I added. "Plastination of bodies, almost two hundred years ago. Absolutely brilliant. Are they still based in Philly?"

"Last I heard, yea. They won a big endowment last fall to help fund them through…" but instead of continuing, Aaron stopped mid-sentence, and reached over to a table and grabbed a Ferrin glove so he could 'touch' the hologram. He lifted the left arm, and held up the hand, which had been clasped in a tight fist when the body was scanned. Now, with the skin and fat removed, we could see the victim had *something* held in his hand.

"Computer; release rigor protocols, and relax the tendons in the left hand," I commanded. The image immediately complied, and another of the creepy crucifixes dropped from the hand into Aaron's Ferrin glove.

"I'll be damned, Ellie. We've been dealing with this cult the whole time!"

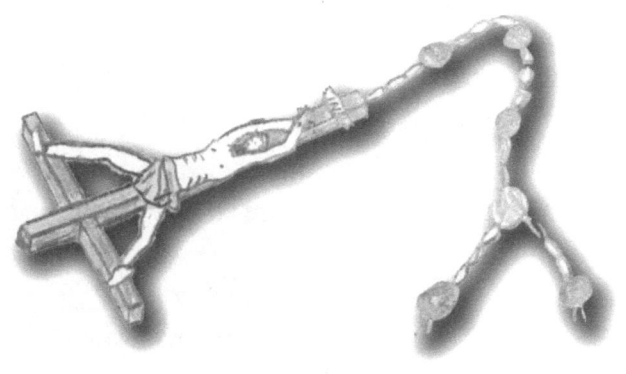

\*\*\*\*\*\*\*\*

"Ok, Ellyandra," Director Forrest said, reviewing the images we'd uncovered in the holo morgue. "This one is nearly identical to the one you recovered from Passenger 303. Does it match up with the one from your new friend from Yucca Mountain?"

"Yes, sir," I answered, pulling up another image to display in front of Jim. "We've done 400x magnification on the image scans, and these are the exact same; the only difference is in the tool marks where the little silver Jesus was mounted to the brass Cross".

"So these were made using the same mold, made by hand. Interesting. Not a lot of people do that kind of work these days".

Just then, Zimmerman walked in, and threw a display paper on the desk in front of Forrest. "They just might do things the old fashioned way if they are a bunch of kooks".

Forrest slid through the images on the display paper quickly, then set the page down on his desk and hit a few buttons to project the display over his desk so we could all see what Zim had found.

"What is all this, Zim?" I asked, trying to soak it all in. "What the hell is a Preterist?"

"An Ultra-Preterist, to be exact, Ellie". Zim flipped the info back to its beginning. "This 'Crucifix', as we've been calling it, is a calling card for a group of 'Ultra-Preterist' that was last known to be based in Baton Rouge, Louisiana. Of course, most of the intel is a few years old, and these cults move around a lot, so they could be anywhere".

"Zim," Michaels said stoically, "We *are* anywhere. We are in the middle of nowhere, in the desert. We've now seen these things in Mobile, in a wrecked plane in old New Orleans, and in Nevada".

"Well, multiple places does still count as anywhere, Aaron", Zim answered back, not missing a beat.

"Zimmerman," Director Forrest interjected. "Stop for just a second, and tell me just what the hell is a 'Preterist'?"

"Well, sir," Zim finally sat down in one of the office chairs and started to prop his feet on the desk. Forrest gave him a scowl that almost made *me* want to run away, and Zim immediately sat back up properly.

"Uhm… you know the Book of Revelation, right?"

"Zimmerman, I am a black man raised in the Deep South; trust me when I say I know 'all' the books of the Bible; and *double* that on Revelation".

"Ok, good. It's all pretty simple, really. Most Christians think of Revelation, and the Second Coming, the Tribulations, etc, as things that are *going* to happen. Preterist think that they all happened almost two millennia ago".

Forrest raised an eyebrow, but only said, "But you said Ultra-Preterist. What's the difference?"

"Honestly, sir... I'm not really clear on that. I'm a Jew; Christianity is a close cousin, but I'd know a lot more if all of this was about the Talmud or if it were a discussion of Rashi's Writings".

"Zim, you found all this on the dark web, right?" He nodded, so I continued. "Has any of it been updated recently? Any recent intel on this particular sect?"

"Well, yeah. That's kinda what got the Government in trouble in the first place. We had Intel on *everyone*. Most of the data files on the servers are dated within the last year, so whatever the courts told them to stop doing, they are still doing it". Zim flipped through a few files, and brought up a new image. "This particular image, of Christ, right side up, on a reversed cross, is tied to a sect led by a man named Jeremiah Power".

"That's a stupid name," Aaron said. Forrest shot another scowl in his direction, but Zim continued.

"According to court records, his given name was Jerry Slate, but he had it changed in 2049 to Jeremiah Power. That's the same year he started preaching his 'message'".

"Ok, Zim. I'll bite," I said, reaching over and grabbing the display paper he'd given Forrest so I could give it a closer look. "Just what is this 'message' that Jeremiah Power has been told to bring to the world?"

"Ever heard of the Horsemen?"

I nodded, waiting for him to continue. On the display paper, I scanned through til I found images of Pestilence, War, Famine and Death, as depicted in various books and movies.

"You can't be serious, Zim? Do people still believe this stuff is literal?" Michaels asked. He looked over to me, but I just nodded back towards Zim so he could continue.

"Some do, yes. And of those, some have been found by Reverend Power. And according to his message, even though the tribulation happened millennia ago, it's taken the Horsemen all this time to do their work. And only one's work remains unfulfilled".

"Death" I said quietly. "They are worshiping Death".

"Not exactly, Ellie. The sect still considers themselves followers of Christ; hence, the odd Crucifix. But according to the report, they see their role in fulfilling prophecy as 'helping the Lord's servant".

"And according to Revelation," Forrest jumped back in, "The Lamb of God broke the seals that released them. The Horsemen *could* be considered servants of God".

"Making these Ultra-Preterist also able to see themselves as servants of God's servants, willing to do *anything* that Jeremiah Power tells them God told him to do".

"And they have dangerous, radioactive material now," Michaels said.

"And," I added, "they have Charles McFarlane; a mind smart enough that he could do absolutely *anything* with that material".

\*\*\*\*\*\*\*\*

We stayed in Vegas for four days, hoping that we could find some trace of the men who'd kidnapped Charles, and blown up the Yucca Mountain facility, but there was no trail. We had only a weird piece of Jewelry to look for, and aside from that, no other identifying information. Finally, late on Sunday, Zim reported that Charles McFarlane's credentials had been used at a secluded, private rest stop entering Louisiana; a fingerprint scan had been captured as well. For whatever reason, they'd taken him back to the South.

After that, we lost the trail. There was no trace, no sign... no anything. All we could do was go home, and keep digging.

\*\*\*\*\*\*\*\*

# 17
## ❧Espionage❧

We had a lot to discuss on the way back to Mobile. Instead of flying, we took a passenger train from Vegas, then on to Bronson, Houston, and across to Pensacola. Since that put us just an hour outside of Mobile, we figured that was close enough, and settled in for the ride. During the trip home, we met, reviewed and planned our next move.

My first job on reaching Mobile was to contact Granddaddy and give him the all clear to come home. Now that we knew what we were looking for, I could actually have him better protected if he was back in Mobile. That and I missed my girls. When I called, they hadn't heard from me for a couple of days, and while that doesn't seem like much for a grown up, it is an E T E R N I T Y for both little girls and stuffed rabbits. While both promised they had known I was OK because "JJ hadn't called them", I realized for the first time that, despite all my assurance that I would be fine, and always come home, my girls knew better. At some level, even at five years old - they knew. And it worried them. I told them both I loved them, and would see them when they got home, then cried for ten minutes because I felt like a failure to them. Unless you've ever really been responsible for young lives like theirs, it's almost impossible to tell you why. I knew better; I knew I'd literally saved them both from a life of torture and cruelty on the black market. I knew that there was nothing I wouldn't do to protect them - even give my own life to see they were safe. But as a parent, there were moments when that still wasn't enough. I didn't want my girls to know that until they were old enough to understand, but those moments come at the oddest times. And like a wave in the ocean, you can let it crash against you, or find a way to ride it to a safe place.

Now, my second job was to head to the Cathedral of the Immaculate Conception. Technically, it was called the **Cathedral Basilica of the Immaculate Conception,** but not being Catholic, I was honestly a little unsure of the *Basilica* part. My

grandfather had suggested that, if I wanted info on
*any* offshoot of Christianity, the best place to start
would be with the original Christian Church. Yea, he
knew that info would be slanted, but he also knew
that the Church had been keeping documents and
information in both libraries and minds for centuries.
So once I made it back home, I contacted the
Archdiocese of Mobile, to make an appointment with
Archbishop Hartley to discuss a little Theology.

The Historic District of Downtown Mobile
had more unique features than I can name off the top
of my head, but the Cathedral on South Claiborne
Street is by far one of the most impressive places I've
ever visited. The place was founded in 1703. It was
one of the first things the Colonist had set up, along
with the Church Street Cemetery. The building itself

wasn't completed until 1850, and had its fair share of bad luck over the last two centuries. Everything from fire and water damage to a WWII pilot clipping one of the towers had befallen this place, but over the years, it had been cleaned, repaired, rebuilt and renovated. It was, simply put, one of the most beautiful places I'd ever visited.

I reached the Cathedral and walked through the iron gates that surrounded the property, up the stairs past the large columns, and through the hand carved double doors into the foyer. The doors that actually allowed entrance into the Sanctuary were actually quite narrow, and while that was less of a problem nowadays, in my Grandfather's time, when people were much bigger, I could see it being an issue. Yet, two centuries had gone by, and while they'd been repaired over the years, these doors had never been replaced. I entered the sanctuary and found it almost empty. It was, after all, a Tuesday afternoon. I'd expected the pews to be empty. But, sitting on the marble steps that led to the pulpit, sat a rotund man, wearing the black vestments of the priesthood, complete with white collar. As I approached, he stood to greet me, hand outstretched.

"Agent Dyett; so good to meet you. I'm Dave Hartley".

I shook the man's hand, commenting, "Ellyandra Dyett; Forgive me, sir, but I expected you to be much more…"

"More what? Formal?" With this, he laughed out loud, letting the joyous sound echo throughout the Sanctuary. "No my dear, I've never been one for formality. I may be an archbishop, but I'm just a man, just another human. I appreciate the honors, but I've no time to stop and worry about titles; I've got bigger fish to fry".

He sat back down on the marble steps, and motioned for me to join him. When I sat, we were facing the Sanctuary, and we sat in a moment of quiet just looking out over the pews, columns, and decorative beauty of the place. Light poured in through Stained Glass Windows on each side, casting beautiful images and multiple colours across both the sanctuary and pulpit.

"They were made in Munich, you know".

"Sir?" I asked gently. This place was quiet: calm. Nothing in me wanted to disturb that feeling.

"The Windows; the stained glass, my dear", he answered, gesturing towards both sides of the sanctuary. "Imported from Munich, Germany in 1890. Been here a long time". The archbishop shifted his bottom on the steps, and turned slightly to face me. "I got your email, and I can tell you the Preterist have been here for a long time, too".

"I'd never heard of them, Sir," I responded, still awestruck at the beauty of this place. "And, with respect," I added carefully, "I've studied a lot of religions in my work".

"You too?" Archbishop Hartley chuckled. "Funny how that works. You work with the dead, and I work with the dying; and we study the same things to help us help them both".

"I'd never really looked at it that way, Sir", I answered. "I never thought of everyone as dying".

"Miss Dyett, we're all dying; we're dying from the moment we are born". The Archbishop stood from the steps, and started walking down the main aisle, gesturing for me to join him, which I did. "Every man, woman and child that lives on this earth is growing, learning, transforming; but eventually, we all die. That's not 'part of the deal' as some would say, it's just a fact. God made this world, in this way, for reasons we may never understand. You can accept it, or fight it, but you'll never truly *change* it'.

The man had a definite ability to make one feel comfortable, even with difficult discussions. Here I was, discussing death, (and in some ways, discussing the absurdity of life, because we all die) with an Archbishop of the Catholic Church in a Cathedral Basilica, and I was as calm as I'd ever been. I might as well have been talking about studying cell samples with Zim and Michaels. Somehow, the man had me totally at ease.

"I can see that. But," I stopped, and he halted his gate so as to not outpace me. "What about these Preterist? They've been labeled 'Ultra-Preterist', but I don't understand. And I *need* to understand, Sir".

"Walk with me, my dear. I have something to show you".

We continued in silence around a few rows of pews, and then cut off to the left towards a spiral staircase that jutted up from the floor. The tiles near the staircase almost felt loose beneath my feet, but the Archbishop assured me that there were no problems, aside from 'age and overuse', so I continued toward the iron staircase, and followed him down.

At the bottom of the stairway, we entered a room, with walls of marble, and a brass gate bisecting the space. On our side of the gate was a marble bench, and on the other side of the gate, I could see the tombs of Archbishops from the past two centuries. Hartley sat on the bench, and patted the remaining space beside him. I joined him, and for a few moments, we sat in silence.

Finally, he spoke. "Preterist, *real* Preterist, believe that it all happened in the past". Before I could interject, he corrected himself. "Well, not everything; not for all of them. That's why you have partial Preterism, and full Preterism. Really, it all boils down to semantics".

"Ok. So, where does that leave us? I asked, hoping for an answer.

The Archbishop gestured across the room, past the brass gate, toward the entombed priest that lay beyond. "Ms. Dyett, do you think *they'd* care about the difference between types of Preterist?"

"If some of their flock were being murdered, yes sir; yes they would".

"Fair enough," he answered, looking haggard, as though he'd been fighting an unseen fight for far too long. "Sometimes - I look at them, the Preterist... and I think they *may* be right".

I started to question, but a quiet, raised hand stopped me. "A lot of what they say matches Scripture. But we both know there is more to it than scripture, don't we?"

I nodded quietly, waiting to see what the man had to say.

"Every man behind that gate has been a shield, my dear. We don't discuss why - they just are. The Preterist we've known may be heretical, but they love God, they love Christ, and even though they have their centuries mixed up, they are not bad people. *One* of the men behind that gate was a Preterist".

"Which one?" I asked, standing to approach the gate and look at the inscribed names on the tombs.

"I like you, Agent Dyett," the Archbishop smiled, "but you'll not be getting all my secrets today. Just know that there are two kinds of Preterist in the Christian faith: the ones that think it's all already happened, and the ones that think *most* of it has happened. There is no such thing as an 'Ultra-Preterist'".

"Then what are these people, who are causing so much trouble and death, and labeling themselves as fighting for God?"

"Ellyandra, you already know," the Archbishop answered, his face suddenly looking tired and serious. "They are what they always are; they're con artist, madmen, and terrorist. They are everything vile and unjust; but they sure as Hell aren't Christians".

********

Aside from talking to the Archbishop, there was a second arm to our plan, but I wasn't a fan of it at all. Jim had come up with the plan on our train ride home. He and Michaels decided the best way to find out what this cult was up to was to find a cell, and infiltrate it. It was a sound plan, and we'd done undercover work before. I knew it was dangerous, but this time, with one friend already missing, and more and more people dying from the *Porcelain Death*, I was downright afraid for them.

Zim had set up all his monitoring equipment so he could keep a constant scan going for Charles' credentials. Now, he added a tracking device scan to follow Jim and Aaron. We tagged both of them with an RFID chip in their buttocks. They already had the tiny comm units in their ear canals, so as long as they didn't lose the control disk, we'd be able to talk. We mocked up some ID cards, credit cards and history, the whole kit and caboodle, so if their backgrounds were checked deeply, they wouldn't lose their cover. Then, off they went, driving off on a mid-June evening, to head towards Louisiana and find the Preterist led by Jeremiah Power.

The first few days of their journey went as planned, and they easily found members of the 'Ultra-Preterist Church' set up in parking lots and parks, sitting in front of speakers and preaching their 'word' to all that were near, whether they wanted to hear it or not. Jim and Aaron decided to split up, so they would attract less attention, and also to more easily find a group to join.

I knew Michaels could pretty much chameleon his way into any group. I'd seen him pull off accents and disguises both planned and improvised, so I wasn't really worried about him as much as I was concerned for Forrest. He'd stayed active in field duties, but hadn't done any undercover work in many years. And despite his appearance, Jim was a lot older than he looked. Of course, I trusted him, and his judgment, enough to go along with the plan. But that didn't mean that I wouldn't worry.

A few days into their mission, we lost the signal on both Aaron and Jim. It was in and out for several days, each tracker moving slowly to opposite ends of the country. Finally, when the signal stabilized, Michaels was in Oregon, and Forrest was in Maine. They were too far away for the comm system to be of any use, so all we could do was watch the grid, follow their signal, and hope that if they needed us, they could somehow get us a signal.

********

It was late August when the deaths started in earnest. Without warning, victims of the *Porcelain Death* started appearing across the country. Victims were found on June 24th; one in Portland, Oregon, another in Bangor, Maine, two outside of San Diego,

California and one more in Homestead, Florida. Zim and I started a national map, marking the new victim's positions, and hoping to hear from Michaels or Forrest soon. More than that, I didn't want to get a report that another victim turned out to be one of them.

By August 30th, we could see a pattern emerge. Every two days since the 14$^{th}$, another set of bodies had been found, and reconnaissance from other Bureau confirmed that a day after each discovery, a group of travelling Preterist came through town.

"Zim," I said, reviewing the large holographic map in Forrest' office, and sipping on coffee. "Jim was in Maine, right?"

"Yep. The last ping we got off his RFID tag put him just outside of Bangor a few weeks ago".

"And Aaron was in Portland".

"Also right. We've gotten a better signal from his implant, and he's shown hits on the grid in Boise, Idaho, Salt Lake City, and Cortez, Colorado".

"OK. Look at our map, Zim". I set my coffee down and hit a few controls to highlight the places we knew Michaels had been. "Here's Aaron's hits. And *here* are the locations of the victims in the Northwest".

"They overlap, El". Zim sat down hard on the desk, adding, "Someone is using the virus victims as breadcrumbs, leading each group of Preterist along their way".

"Question is, my friend, where are they being led?"

\*\*\*\*\*\*\*\*

# 18
## ❧Epiphany❧

Zim set the MR-CSA's to link together and work on projecting a pattern on the placement of the known victims, and we headed off for the night. It was too easy to stay at the office all the time, waiting, hoping for a lead or a new event. Since the bodies had started showing up, I grew more and more fearful that the next one may be one of my boys. And even though he was my boss, when Jim Forrest was undercover like this, he counted as one of my boys.

Granddad and the girls had returned home in late June. So at least that part of my life had been getting back to something that felt normal. Plain clothes officers had been placed in and around my building, and I hadn't seen anyone spying on me in months, so I was finally feeling more at ease in my home than I had in a while. I came home to find that my dear grandfather had once again lolst track of time, going through the hundreds of pictures he and the girls had taken in Vermont. I hugged all three of them, went and changed into pajamas (or 'majamas' as Olivia called them), then went to start dinner and pour myself a glass of wine. Once the food was started, I went back out to find my girls sitting at the dinner table, showing Chester photo after photo. The stuffed rabbit looked intently at each one before giving an approving nod. I just smiled and shook my head slightly, and brought my grandfather a glass of Merlot.

"Looks like they are still going through pics, granddad", I said, sitting close to him on the sofa. "I'm glad you had a good time".

"I always loved Vermont, my dear". He took a small sip and set his glass down on the coffee table. "You know I lived there in my early thirties; almost seven years. Beautiful place, good people. Sometimes I miss them, but," he sat back slowly on the sofa, "too many people I can only visit in the cemetery. Might as well live where it's warm".

"You know the girls adore you. I'm so glad you're here," I said, placing my arm around him and hugging him tightly".

"Like I said, love. Might as well live where it's warm".

********

Dinner was a simple feast of what my mother had always called 'Daddy's World Famous Spaghetti', which of course meant that it was my grandfather's recipe. Over the years he'd offered bits and pieces of his culinary secrets to me, and now, when I cooked this meal, he said it was just as good as his was. I promised him that I'd make sure to teach the girls the family's recipe when they were old enough.

Since it was a Friday night, I let the girls bring all the dishes to the kitchen, then got them in a bath and pajamas, and promised them they could stay up late playing as long as they weren't loud. Each girl came downstairs with an armload of stuffies, Lego's and other toys, and after two such trips, my living room looked like a toy shop had exploded. Granddad sat on the sofa watching them, and I curled up in an armchair with my handheld, and some document images, to look over the case. I found that most nights, I was either in here with my girls playing, or they were on the floor of my study playing while I worked. But no matter what we were all doing, they were near, and that made us all happy.

It was around seven when Zim rang my door. Of course, Erin and Olivia came running through the foyer and nearly tackled him in their excitement, but they quickly settled back down and went back to their games. Apparently, Olivia informed me as she put the toy snorkel and swim trunks back on Chester, the living room was now all underwater, and Chester was going to go diving to see what he could find. I kissed them both on the forehead and returned to my seat, pulling up another chair so Zim and I could talk.

"So, what brings you back to town tonight, Zim?" I said, pulling my feet underneath me, and taking a small drink. "I thought you'd be home by now, snoozing away".

Zim nodded towards my grandfather, who was now peacefully snoring away on the sofa. "You mean like him? Nah, I never sleep that well. Brain's too busy".

"I know that feeling, Zim". I picked up the documents I'd been reviewing, and added, "Plus, it's weird not having Michaels or Forrest around. When did we last hear from them again?"

"We heard from Aaron on Monday. He had a chance to use a library computer and send me an email. It codes just as expected, so anyone else reading it would think he was telling his mom he's ok. As for Jim, his situation is a little worse".

"How so?"

"He knows we can hear him, and he can hear us through the comms, but he gets no time alone, not even to pee. He talks in code out loud so I can hear, but they think he's lost his mind". Zim took a sip of my wine, declaring, "He's doing a very convincing job of sounding insane".

I turned back to my handheld where a street-cam had grabbed an image of Forrest and one of his 'minders' on their way through Pennsylvania. He'd altered his garb to look the part of a street person, and I'd never seen Forrest unshaven or dirty. Even though I knew he was uncomfortable, he was safe. That's all that mattered for now.

"Ellie," Zim asked. "Can I ask you something?"

"Sure, Zim. Anything".

"What made you call it quits with Charles McFarlane?"

While I wasn't expecting that, I couldn't say I was totally surprised either. Ever since Zim had opened up at Yucca Mountain, he'd been, if not withdrawn, at least visibly reflective. I had the feeling that facing those memories had him thinking about a lot of things. Zim and Michaels both had found an even deeper friendship by sharing their feeling about their long dead other halves. Now, it was my turn to offer him what I could, in hopes it would help him find some peace.

I drew a deep breath, and let it slowly out, keeping my own internal stresses in check. "You know he found a cure for blindness, right?" Zim nodded yes. "He was twenty-two. That's awfully young for that kind of success, and with his already 'stellar' personality, it went right to his head. I knew what he was doing was important, so I let it slide. Finally," I said, "it slid too far. I came home one day to a wild party, and found him in a hot tub with three other women, who were either partially clothed or wearing *my* clothes. I was livid. Turns out he was being courted for a position with a pharmaceutical company, and wining and dining was only part of what they offered him. They literally threw gorgeous women at him. Plus, I found out later, that they had laced his food and drink with drugs, so by the time I got home, he was a wasted, drooling mess".

"What did you do, Ellie?"

I took a larger drink from my glass, finishing what was left. "It wasn't what I did, Zim; *I* ran to the guest room, locked the door, and cried myself to sleep".

Zim sat, quietly waiting for me to finish. "*He* got angry; threw everyone out of the house, then proceeded to take all of my belongings and throw them outside. It started pouring right after he tossed everyone out. We were pretty much living together almost full time by then, so when I say he tossed out *everything I owned*, I'm not kidding. Almost every piece of clothing I had was either lost or ruined".

"But he was drugged, Ellie?" Zim said. "When you found that out, did it make a difference?"

"Sometimes, I wish it had. But that night set off a full week of yelling, screaming and hateful insults that made me loathe him; and I daresay he hated me too. Even after he'd come down from the drugs, he was ashamed and embarrassed. Can you imagine someone with Charles' personality being ashamed and embarrassed?"

"I can't imagine that went well at all".

"In the end, he left me," I admitted. "We were both in the wrong, and had both used our closeness as weapons against each other. That's hard to forgive".

"So when you contacted him a few years ago on the Waldorf case?"

"We hadn't spoken in almost five years. Frankly, I'm surprised he helped us. I was even more surprised when he started staying around".

I got up to grab another glass of wine. Remembering those days, when we were both destroying each other and ourselves, was emotionally exhausting. When I came back to the living room, I noticed my girls had built a nearly three-foot-tall stack of toys and stuffed animals, with Chester stuck all the way at the bottom.

"Mamma?" Olivia asked quietly. "Can you ask granddaddy to stop making the motorboat sounds now? We don't need 'em anymore".

"I'll see if I can get granddaddy to head on to bed, loves," I answered, side stepping by the girls construction over to my grandfather, and gently whispering to him that he needed to head on to bed. He got up, hugged me and both girls, and *almost* stopped to hug Zimmerman on his way to the stairs. Once he'd headed off, I sat back down.

"Livy, my love?" I asked, seeing all sorts of cars and trains and boats stuck here and there in their 'underwater city'. "Why is Chester at the bottom?"

Erin jumped in, eager to answer. "That's silly, Mamma. Chester's at the bottom because he found it first!"

"Yeah," Olivia said excitedly. "Once everyone else came, they built the City around him!"

Just under Chester's left foot, I saw a toy submarine, stuck securely between my living room rug and his bedraggled worn paw. "What about the sub, my loves?"

"That's how Chester got there, Mamma. It was too deep for him to swim".

"And just *where* did Chester get a Submarine, my darlings?" I asked.

"He just found it, Mom!". Olivia and Erin looked at each other, then back to me shaking their heads. "We don't know *where*".

I sat back to let the girls play, but I kept looking at the toy submarine. It looked like a similar design to the sub we'd been on last year.

"I wish it was easy to just find a submarine," Zim said, yawning slightly.

"Zim," I said, unable to stop thinking of the missing sub that I knew had sent men after me and my family. I reached down to pick up the tiny toy, and had an inspiration. "I think I know where to find the MURDERER'S SLAVE, and it's been right under our noses the whole time".

\*\*\*\*\*\*\*

# 19
### ❧Counterpoint❧

Saturday turned into a work day, with Zim set up in my study researching old New Orleans, and me bouncing back and forth between spending time with my girls and helping Zim research the sunken city. Once we were looking at the data, it seemed like an obvious fit. Most of the guided dives of the ruins had been canceled due to 'hazardous conditions'. Turns out that each of the major dive crews had people that had literally disappeared on the guided tour over the last few months, and they were all shutting down until they could figure out where these people had gone.

Above the water, the ring of collapsed buildings and broken roadways that once led into the city had attracted a new type of settler. Local police departments reported that the disenfranchised from all over the south had started to make 'camp' in the old ruins. Like the Dark Zones, the Ruins of New Orleans were considered non-property, so the police and governments stayed away, content to let the non-landowning, non-voting poor either live or die, without a care in the world for their well being.

I took a few moments to assign a recovery drone to the settlement, just as a precaution. I also sent a dive camera to scout around a few well known areas like the French Quarter and the Garden District. Even though the area had been well documented by divers for many years, sometimes it's a good idea to get a look at how things are in the here and now, instead of relying on images that could be several years old.

After lunchtime, and a decent afternoon nap, Zim and I started reviewing the dive drone footage. When New Orleans fell, it fell hard and fast. A great chasm had been created under the city, and that space was now filled with a litter of debris, buildings, and broken infrastructure. Massive piles of rubble created artificial rises, dark narrow ravines, and places that were almost impossible to see into. But there on the screen, we could easily see that some of the sunken buildings were lit from within. And underneath these lights, although it was almost totally obscured, we could barely see the tail end of what looked like a submarine.

Zim fiddled with the images for an hour, but even with his level of skill, there was no cleaning up the dark grainy mess that we had.

"This is not going well," Zim offered, sitting back from my terminal and grabbing a water from the tiny fridge in the study. "There's just too much crap in the water. If the cameras on the dive drones were better, then *maybe* I'd have more to work with".

"There's only one way to know for sure, Zim. We've got to go and dive it ourselves"

He nodded slowly, turning his attention to a beep on his handheld. "Looks like the MR-CSA's have finished their calculations, Ellie". He punched up a map of the US over my desk, pulled the data from the system, and highlighted the movement of the four groups of Preterist from the four corners of the country. "The blue shows their known path. The red shows the projections".

It was staring us in the face. There were a few red projections that went off to nowhere, but with almost no deviation, all four paths crossed in the same area.

"Ellie, Zim observed, "Eighty-eight percent of the possible destinations for the Preterist groups intersect over old New Orleans".

\*\*\*\*\*\*\*\*

Knowing where the Preterist were headed was a game-changer. It meant that we could pull Michaels and Forrest out, and add anything they'd learned to what we knew. But before we could do that, we had to find them. I left my Grandfather with the girls, gave Mom an extra set of keys since we'd had all the locks changed, and alerted building security to be more vigilant since neither me, nor my boys would be in town. Since the mariners who'd invaded my home had each had one of the Preterist Crucifixes, we knew they were linked, so I also assigned more plainclothes officers to watch my family while I was gone.

After making sure things were as secure as we could get them, Zim headed west, using the RFID tracking info and the computer's projections in hopes of meeting Michaels somewhere in Texas. I headed northeast, hoping to intercept Forrest's group somewhere either in eastern Tennessee, or possibly Virginia. We had a lot of good information to go on, but the route was still huge, and the groups weren't being led on the major roadways; it was a shot in the dark at best.

It took Zimmerman almost two weeks to locate the group that Michaels was with. They'd just stopped outside of Abilene, Texas a day after another *Porcelain Death* victim had been found, and Zim was close enough to arrive at the same time as they did. This group spread throughout the City in pairs, passing out flyers and handing out the kind of little comics that had scared the crap out of me as a child. 'Evangelical Tracts' they had been called, each one designed to prey upon your fear in order to save your soul.

Before they had headed out, we had come up with several extraction ideas to use when the time came. Because of Forrest having a minder, all those plans were off. Michaels, on the other hand, had at least half a dozen ways that he and Zim had devised. When Michaels wandered up to Zimmerman in Satterfield's Park, he pretended not to know him, and walked right into him in a careless, yet obvious attempt to pick his pockets. As he did so, Zim placed a spare wallet in Michaels' coat pocket, calling out to some well-placed police officers when the 'theft' was discovered a few moments later. From what I heard, Michaels' acting skills were right on the mark, and he made a huge scene, drawing the attention of the Preterist in the area, as well as a large crowd. He struggled and fought with the officers, screaming all the while that 'death's work would be visited upon the world soon!', as they cuffed him and shoved him in a squad car.

It was the perfect extraction. Michaels was 'interrogated, processed, and *transferred*' to a facility outside of Abilene, all in one afternoon. From there, Zim picked him up, and the two started back towards Mobile.

I wasn't having such an easy time. By following the news of new *Porcelain Death* victims, I was able to be ready when Forrest' group hit Knoxville. But unlike the group that Michaels was with, *this* group wasn't in town to do any evangelizing; they were here to see the bodies, and until they could find that opportunity, they hid.

I was now close enough to Forrest' position that I could talk to him by way of the tiny comm unit we'd hidden in his ear. I opened the channel to listen, and gently whispered, "Jim. It's Ellie. I'm close. Can you find a way to tell me where you are?"

What Forrest did next was an act of pure genius. He didn't even try to hide his answer. He almost yelled, "Hey there! We're in K N O X V I L L E! Haha! Gonna have a *good* time here! Lots of people here; lots of *work* to do!" His voice had gone from excited to almost a low growl with his last statement, and just for a moment, I wondered if we'd lost him. Deep cover jobs around religious zealots were dangerous. Sometimes, people really did get pulled in, never to be seen again. "Now, ladies and gentlemen! When are we gonna see the Martyrs?!"

There was an uproar around him. It was loud enough that I had to turn the volume down until it subsided. "Jim, you need to tell me where you are".

A moment of silence was finally broken, when he said, "Church. We're *always* at church, RIGHT THOMAS!" I heard a voice shouting an affirmative, followed by Forrest muttering, "Church, Church, Church; oh yea, ALWAYS at Church!" over and over again. I could feel tears starting to build in my eyes. I couldn't believe it, but it sounded like Forrest really had gone crazy.

"Cordova; BIG Church", Jim continued, going from loud to quiet. "Big church, but no one here; no one around anymore. Headed HOME after we see the Martyrs! HEADED HOME!"

"Jim, you've got to tell me where to find you!" I said, still whispering, even though I knew no one else could hear me.

"Cordova! Big Church; no one here," he said.

I pulled up a list of churches in and around Knoxville, but didn't find anything on Cordova. Then, I added closed and abandoned churches to the search, and I hit the jackpot.

"First Baptist of Cordova. Closed ten years ago, been empty ever since. That's gotta be it."

"YES! YES, LORD SHE UNDERSTANDS!" Forrest yelled. There was more cheering around him.

"I'm coming to get you, Jim. Hang tight".

\*\*\*\*\*\*\*\*

It was dark by the time I reached the abandoned church, but it was easy to see why the cult had chosen this place. It was close to Knoxville's Dark Zone, which also put it fairly close to police headquarters. I'd been listening to Forrest through the commlink on my way, and heard that the group was planning on finding the victims of the *Porcelain Death* that had been discovered here, and taking them away as holy relics. I found a place to secure my transport, crossed the decaying fence, and worked around the perimeter of the building until I could get inside.

"Jim. I'm here. Where are you?"

He muttered 'sanctuary', followed by, "THOMAS! I GOTTA PEE!"

Suddenly, I could hear 'Thomas' yelling, "Don't pee behind the pulpit! That's a sacred space!" Forrest was laughing, and it was all I could do to not laugh out loud. I had pulled up a schematic of the building before I arrived, so I was able to make my way quietly to the Sacristy, which was basically behind the pulpit. If I could make my way there, I could hide until I had a chance to grab Forrest. Up until now, I was lucky I'd been able to avoid the guards, but as soon as I entered the small room, I saw Jim leaning forward against a wall, urinating, and there was a rough-looking man with him. He had a pistol pointed at Jim's head. I leveled my pulser and triggered the new taser-like setting, dropping him before he could react.

Forrest tidied himself, turned around and grabbed me in a big bear hug.

"Jim, you smell awful," I commented, the mix of filth and body odor almost overwhelming me.

"Missed you too, Ellie," he said with a smile. "This group isn't big on baths".

I handed Jim a pulser I'd brought for him, just in case we had to fight our way out, but he tucked it under his jacket, and picked up Thomas' gun instead. "This will be more convincing, Ellyandra".

We tried our best to sneak back the way I'd come, but this time, my timing was off, and we walked around a corner in the back hallways and almost ran into a well-armed guard. He leveled a high-powered rifle at me, and then looked to Forrest. Jim held his pistol to my side.

"What's this?" the guard asked. "Somebody got nosey, eh?"

"Taking her to Thomas," Jim answered, digging the gun roughly into my side. "He'll want to talk to this one".

"The guard waved us past, but just after we got around him, he said, "Wait a minute. Thomas is *your* minder. Where is he?"

"Aw, hell, buddy. You got me!" Forrest said as he turned around, and cold cocked the guard with the pistol. I kicked the guards' gun away from where he'd fallen, and we ran.

We made it to the fence before they sounded an alarm, and just got to the transport as the gun-wielding fanatics rounded the corner. We sped off in the opposite direction, alerting the Knoxville Police Department of the cult's location. What they did with them now was none of our business. As for me and my boss - my friend - we would stop at the first safe hotel so Jim could get a shower. There was no way in hell I could take that stench for hours trapped in a car together.

********

## 20
### ❧Abduction❧

That night was the first safe night's sleep Forrest had gotten in weeks. As soon as we were far enough away from the cult, the first thing Jim did was to call his wife. He was actually in tears when he heard her voice, but he kept his calm, saying "Hello, baby. Daddy's comin' home". I could hear Sandra over the comm, in tears and squealing with joy. She'd been a bureau wife longer than I'd been alive. I knew she had at one time been used to Jim going undercover for weeks, even months at a time. But going back to that mindset, especially as you age, must've been a damned difficult thing to do. It really made me think about things.

The next morning, I exited my motel room to see Jim waiting for me by the transport. He'd bathed, showered, bathed *again,* and shaved his face and head. Even though his usual suit coat and tie were nowhere to be seen, this was the Jim Forrest I knew and admired. I went up to him and hugged him again, commenting, "OK. Now you don't smell like death. That's more like it!"

"I should give the motel owners a bonus to cover all the water I used last night," Forrest said, gently patting my back. "I just didn't feel like I could get clean". Then, as he took a step back, he became suddenly solemn. "The rhetoric was... dangerous, Ellie. There were moments, when... when I wasn't sure I was acting anymore". I opened the transport passenger door and motioned for him to sit, then hopped into the driver's seat.

"Computer; take us back to Mobile". I commanded. Since this was a Federal transport, it didn't have an AI with a personality, so it simply complied with a beep, and started moving us down the road.

"How did you deal with it, Jim?" I asked, turning to face him. He sat with his head down, looking at his hands in his lap.

"I think pretending to be crazy actually helped me. It kept me grounded, knowing it was all an act. But," he shook his head a bit, "but they *weren't* acting. They were for real". Forrest motioned toward a fast food joint, and I grabbed the wheel, taking control from the AI. I didn't bother to ask him what he wanted; I already knew. We'd worked together long enough that we both could take care of each other, without missing a beat. I almost ordered his usual, then paused, and looked at the man. I saw weeks on a hunger diet that had robbed him of pounds and muscle; I saw a man who was trying hard to not be shell-shocked as he returned to a normal life. I saw my friend, desperately trying to hold it together, when I knew I'd heard him crying off and on throughout the night.

"Order, Ma'am?" the attendant asked, patiently waiting.

"Two coffees, black. One with light cream. One breakfast sandwich, and..." I looked over to Forrest, who was still watching his hands in his lap. "One egg and cheese biscuit, please". Normally,

Forrest would have had a much more substantial breakfast, even if we had been forced to eat fast food. For now, I knew that if we put too much in his stomach, it would come right back with a vengeance. His system would take a few days at least to start getting back to normal. His mind would react, and he'd put on a good face for all of us. But I knew better. I knew there would be light duty, where he'd ask me to fill out papers I usually had to bring to him. There would be days where he took an extra day here and there for 'personal time'. I knew there would be counseling, and therapy, to help him deal with all he'd seen, and all he'd had to do to survive. That was the nature of the job, and we all knew it. But we all secretly hoped that we'd not have to go in too deep anywhere, for the sake of our sanity. I'd been lucky in Miami; I had found a place to hide on a daily basis, a small place where I could put my back to a corner, be alone, and fall asleep on guard, so I didn't truly have to live it twenty-four/seven - not like Jim had. Forrest had been watched since the first moment, and there was no letting up, no single second of escape. If that is how this particular sect of the Ultra-Preterist treated all their new inductees, there was no wondering why they were all nuts. No one, no man or woman, can take that level of scrutiny, for that long.

Forrest seemed relieved that I wasn't force-feeding him like my grandmother used to feed me during summer vacation. I could have doted on him minute by minute, stuffing him with food and drink, and coddling him, but in some ways, he'd already been through that with the Preterist. What Forrest needed now, right in that instant, was solitude. And while I couldn't give him that, I could offer him gentle encouragements, and my silence. He'd talk to me when (and if) he wanted to. I knew the man inside, who'd been an Agent for decades, would give up any pertinent information without hesitation. But, like Zimmerman and his deceased fiancée', I needed to wait until Forrest *wanted* to tell me the details.

That's what friends do. Always.

\*\*\*\*\*\*\*\*

We had just passed Montgomery when Forrest spoke again. "Ellie, where are we on things?" Before I could answer, he asked, "Did you pull me out because I was losing it?"

I didn't respond at first. I had to stop and really think about what I was about to tell him. I knew he deserved the truth, but I was worried about the impact it could have on him.

"Jim, until I came for you, we could hardly follow you". I didn't put in any emphasis, I just said it. It was the truth, as much as I hated it. "Something went wrong with tracking and comms, but by the time we discovered it, you were too far in to pull you out safely".

We drove on for two miles before Forrest answered, "Good call, Ellie". I looked over to my boss to see him visibly sweating, but there was no other reaction. A few miles later, he said, "But you never really lost me, did you? I mean…"

"Only for a few hours at a time". I answered honestly. He deserved the whole truth. "Zim and I monitored a team of agents who had helped keep track of your transmissions, but they were in and out". Forrest eyes seemed to be searching far ahead of him as I continued, "But we always knew you were safe. We knew you were acting crazy, so everything we heard, we passed through that filter".

Jim sat in the seat next to me, trying hard to maintain emotional control. "El… Ellyandra. I knew I was in good hands. Sorry I gave you any…trouble".

The ride home had given him something he'd not had in weeks. It gave him time to think, and let the reality of it all sink in. The realization that he had *really* been alone, that the safety net of the tracking devices and commlink had gaping holes, that knowledge had him thinking in circles. And it was a dangerous path to start on. I passed driving control back to the autonomous vehicle, and turned the seat to face my friend. "We're not military, but... permission to speak freely, Sir?"

Jim nodded, with an almost glazed look on his face.

"Sir, you are my boss; you have led and directed me for years, and I appreciate everything you have done for me and my family". Forrest looked over to me, so I continued, "But you are also my friend and comrade, so for god's sake, snap out of it!"

Forrest sat in the passenger's seat, still looking dazed and somewhat lost, so I continued. "You were OK this morning, and you can be OK now. You are thinking TOO MUCH, damn it!" I quickly followed myself with a "Sir".

Jim looked at me, and I could see what his mind had been going through the whole trip. He tried to face it all at once, to get it behind him, so he could be one-hundred percent when we got home. But this wasn't something he could just shake off, logically deal with, and relegate to the back of his mind to deal with later. This was fresh blood, far too recent to ignore, and far too *raw* to simply put aside.

"Jim, you know we love you. You know we *need* you. But you can't help us, unless you let us know what *you* need". Forrest started to protest, but I just rolled on. "*You* would tell me the same thing, am I right?" I asked, waiting for an answer. A moment passed, but he slowly nodded an affirmative, so I kept going, "OK; you eventually want to retire? To have me as a Director one day?" Forrest shook his head yes again, still silent, but with a more confident motion this time. "Then, SIR," I started, reaching out to grab his face and *make* him look directly at me, "You'd better be prepared to get what you give!" He looked puzzled in his silence, so I added, "You take care of us; so we take care of *you!*"

He didn't speak again until we hit Evergreen, AL, halfway between Montgomery and Mobile. We were almost home, when he straightened his shirt, sat up in his seat, and said, "Ellyandra, you're right'.

Before I could even add or ask anything, he continued, "So, where are we with these 'Preterist'?"

\*\*\*\*\*\*\*\*

It took me the better part of an hour to catch Jim up on all we'd learned about the Preterist sect, and its connections to not only the people who'd been killed by the *Porcelain Death*, but the Pirates, the Crucifixes, and the terrorist threat of the virus connected to the disappearance of Charles McFarlane. It took him a bit to come around, and catch the connections we'd made.

"So, the Pirates that attacked you had the Preterist' Crucifixes, so we can assume they've been absorbed by the cult?"

"Yes, sir," I answered. "And the Pirate sub had been seen around Norway, where there was an old RWX Corp office. Charles said he found the structure for the virus in their records".

"Hmm; that's likely how they got their hands on the virus to begin with," Forrest agreed. "But why would the Preterist want to work with a group of Pirates?"

"That's one of the holes, and believe me, there are still plenty". We started crossing the 'General W.K. Wilson Bridge', (a large, dual arch bridge that almost everyone in lower Alabama simply called the 'Dolly Parton Bridge'), and finally hit Mobile County on its other side. This was the last leg of our long trip. "I still don't know why the Pirates came after me to begin with".

Forrest stretched as best as he could in the small transport. "That isn't a hole, Ellyandra. That is a big, gaping, dangerous void; and I don't like it at all".

"Me either, Sir", I said, turning back to the wheel and taking control from the computer. "I don't like it at all".

\*\*\*\*\*\*\*\*

We met Sandra Forrest at the Federal Building in Downtown Mobile. She was a tall woman, with a smiling face and wisps of grey in her long, flowing hair. She nearly dropped Jim as he got out of the transport, and he in turn held onto her so tight you could almost see them melding together. They quietly held onto each other for several long moments, before finally separating enough for Sandra to thank me for bringing him home. The Forrests walked away together, and seeing them just made me smile. Love like that is a gift, and it's a gift that too few ever find.

I took a monorail to the carpark on Broad Street, and found my car, my 'Deloris', just where I'd left her. As I got inside, I reached to my pocket to pull out my comm unit, and noticed that the battery had drained on the trip home. I set the unit on the dash to charge, and Deloris asked, "Hi Ellie. Did you have a nice trip?"

"I wouldn't call it nice, Deloris," I answered, waiting for her AI to finish booting up from sleep mode. "But I brought my friend home, so it was worth it".

"Ellie," Deloris commented. "I see your communications and data unit has suffered total power loss. While I charge it, shall I check your messages? I've been asleep while you were away".

I laid the seat back, hitting the buttons to allow Deloris complete control on the drive home. "Please. Let's see what I missed".

"You have three non-text messages". Deloris immediately started playing the first one, and I sat up as soon as I heard the voice. *"El, its mom. Call me".*

"Deloris," I asked. "Are the other messages from mom, too?"

"Only one. Shall I continue?"

I nodded, knowing that Deloris could see as well as hear me.

*"Ellie, its mom. The girls are ok, but... something's happened. I'm calling the police. I'll see you when you get home".*

That last part hit me square in the gut. There was only one or two reasons that mom would be meeting me at my house.

"Deloris! Get us home NOW!" I commanded. Her AI complied, tapping into the computer systems that ran the street traffic, and opening pathways in the roads that no human could have navigated. I was doing at least 100 MPH down Airport Blvd, weaving in and out, seeing lights change and other traffic holding back, just to let us through. If I hadn't been scared for my family, I might have been scared for myself. But I had too much on my mind, too many fears running amuck, releasing deamon after deamon in the back of my head, to even care or question my own safety. I just needed to get home.

When we pulled up to *The Rose*, I jumped out of Deloris and ran to the doors, hitting the lift in record time, and almost coming out of my skin waiting to travel the 125 floors to my apartment. I squeezed through the doors as they finally opened, running down the hallway to my apartment home. MPD had a man posted at my door, but I went right past him, into my living room, to find my mother sitting with a little girl on each leg, coddling them, and rocking gently.

"MAMMA!" they yelled in stereo, both hopping down from my mother's lap, and running toward me, almost jumping into my arms. I knelt down to hug them close, and looked up to my mother. She looked tired; more tired than I'd ever seen her. Her eyes were a give-away that she'd been crying, and taking a look at my girls, I could see they'd been crying too. There were a few police officers standing around, comparing notes, and then, I could see it.

"Mom? Where's Granddaddy?" I asked. The girls started crying again. Mom started crying again. I felt my own tears welling up in my eyes. He was an old man; anything was possible.

"Mom?" I asked again, but it was Erin who answered. "They took him, Mamma".

"We couldn't stop them. We screamed and yelled, but we're too little!" Olivia added through her tears.

My mother sat beside me on the floor of my living room, taking Erin into her arms, so I could fully embrace Olivia. I just looked at her with longing. I needed to know. Finally, after what felt like an eternity, Mom bowed her head for a moment, visibly gathering her strength, then sat up straight, and looked at me. "Daddy's been kidnapped, love. We don't know where he is".

\*\*\*\*\*\*\*\*

I was really grateful for the Mobile County Police Department. With two-thirds of my team out of town, (three-quarters if you counted the missing Charles McFarlane), and my boss needing time to recover, I felt more alone than I had since I'd sat strapped in a chair in the Dark Zone, waiting to be murdered, with only my own shattered voices to keep me company. As much as I needed to get all the details, my girls needed me more. So we sat together for an hour, just cuddling while they cried, and I tried my best to not let them see my tears. I couldn't afford to fall apart now. Not if I was going to be of any use to my girls, my mother, or my grandfather.

After the girls calmed down enough for mom to take them to their room to rest, I went to the Detective I'd seen earlier in my living room. He'd been patiently waiting for me by the dining room table, wise enough to not interrupt the time my babies needed with me.

"Thanks for that," I said, reaching out a hand. "They've been through too much already in their lives; they needed me".

"I read the report, Miss Dyett. Detective Steven Benson. Your mother gave me a lot of background. I knew what you needed to do".

I lowered my head, then looked around my home while I declared, "And I know your boys are doing their part, so I'm not worried about that. But, if you could fill me in, I'd appreciate it".

"Of course" Detective Benson pulled out a chair for me, but I grabbed the one I usually sat in and motioned for him to take a seat. "Late yesterday evening, your grandfather had taken Erin and Olivia to West Mobile Park. The girls said that he wanted to get them some fresh air and sunshine". I nodded, knowing that sounded exactly like my grandfather. "We've got better statements from a few people who were at the park. Your family was together when two unidentified men came out of the bushes, hit your grandfather with a taser, and carried him off to a waiting car. From what we've been able to discern, it took all of a minute".

"Vehicle description?" I asked, "Plate number? And Security transmit codes to the grid?"

"Nothing. Even the people who witnessed the abduction said that the car wasn't like any cars they'd seen before. Just a 'boxy, small thing with wheels'".

"What did the girls say, when you asked them?"

"We didn't" Detective Benson answered. "They're five years old. Nothing they say is admissible in court".

I stood up, trying not to shout, "We're not *in* court, you dolt!" Immediately, I started walking towards the stairs, adding, "Those kids have seen too much, been through too much, to *not* be able to give us some detail that we've missed. Admissible or not," I growled, topping the stairs and reaching for the doorknob of their room, "they can tell us what we're missing".

********

I was a very lucky mother, not because my girls always behaved, or never did wrong. To the contrary, they were just as mischievous and daring as I was at that age. No, I was lucky because between the three of us, there was perfect trust, and no secrets. And that, my friends, is a truly rare gift, that *all* parties have to be on board with, or it just doesn't work. I knew that asking the girls to relive granddad's abduction would be traumatic to them. I also knew that if I didn't include them, they'd always wonder what they might have been able to do to help. That's just who they were. So I calmly went into their room, whispered in my mother's ear what I needed to do, and sat down to 'play' with my beautiful daughters.

After a few minutes of fiddling about with action figures they'd glued glitter and batwings to, Erin and Olivia looked at me, and said, "Mamma, we know you're worried". Olivia patted me on the back, and Erin gently stroked my hair out of my face. "You don't have to play if you don't want to," Olivia added, with Erin answering, "I don't want to play, Livy. I want to find granddaddy!"

"Me neither!" Olivia said, reaching over to her sister, and grabbing her hand.

"Me either, my loves," I said, putting my hand over theirs. "But loves, not a lot of people saw what happened".

The girls looked at each other, then back to me, both saying "BUT WE DID, MAMMA!"

"We saw it!" Erin shouted.

"All of it!" Olivia responded. She then held up Chester, adding "Chester saw it too!"

I gave Detective Benson a sideways glance, and a small smile. "Ok, my loves. Can you tell me what you saw?"

"Mamma," Erin started. It was awful".

"We were throwing a Frisbee with granddaddy,

Detective Benson interjected, "Isn't he their *great* granddad?"

"They *are* five; cut em some slack, ok?" I said. "So, my loves," turning back to my girls, "where were we?"

"Chester threw the Frisbee, Mamma" Olivia said, holding their stuffed rabbit up in the air.

"He did?"

"Yeah! And Granddaddy had to *run* to get it" Olivia answered.

"Well, run as best as he could, Livy; he is, like, nine hundred years old!" Erin interjected.

"No, Sweetie; that's Yoda," I said, playing along with the joke. "Granddaddy is only two hundred years old".

"But Mamma, that's when the mean men grabbed him!" Erin said, almost starting to cry again.

"They hit him with a stick, Mamma" Olivia said, grabbing her sister's hand again. "It had a little 'boomp', and then granddaddy fell down!"

I knew that the abductors had to have tazed my grandfather, so even with the girls limited ability to describe what they'd seen, filtering what they said through the eyes of a little girl, it matched.

"I should have chased them, Mamma," Olivia said. She clutched Chester tightly. "But I was too scared".

"I was too, 'Livia," Erin answered, grabbing hold of her sister and their shared stuffed rabbit.

"Loves, you did *all* you could. You are only five years old, my loves". I hugged my babies tight for another minute, allowing the tears they needed, and even letting Erin wipe her nose on my shirt. Once they'd settled down a bit, I asked a leading question.

"Sweethearts, can you tell me anything about the men?" My girls looked at me blankly, so I added, "Like, can you tell me what they were wearing?"

I knew I was asking a lot of them, and I hated myself for doing it. But I knew my girls, and I knew how strong and smart they really were (not just in my eyes as their mom, but 'really'... how others had seen them). Erin and Olivia snuggled close together, holding Chester between them. I'd seen this before, but this wasn't a 'shut it down' signal. This was the way they protected themselves, in hard times. When they were unsure, their velveteen protector stepped in, and spoke for them.

"Loves," I asked, getting their eyes, and their attention. "Did they have uniforms?"

Olivia grabbed Chester by the back of the neck, and made him nod a 'yes'.

I reached for my comm, finding that Deloris had only been able to give it a ten percent charge on the trip home. I pulled up a picture of the uniforms of the pirates that had invaded my home a few months before, and held it up for the girls to see. I didn't even have to ask. They each flinched back, holding Chester between them and the image, as soon as I showed them. I had the answer that I needed.

I put the comm back in my pocket, and opened my arms. My girls came flooding into my open lap, and I held them tight. The four of us, (if you counted Chester) sat together for a few minutes, and I could feel when my girls had actually settled down. The hour was late, so I carried them both in my arms to their beds. Clothes could be changed tomorrow. For now, they needed sleep, but what they'd given me was an assertion of what I'd already feared. The Pirates had not come for me this time. They'd found another way to get to me. But I still didn't know why *I* was one of their targets.

Now the Preterist had my former fiancée, and the Pirates had my grandfather. I could only hope that we were right in thinking they were working together. If they were, we just might find them in the same place.

If I wasn't right, they were both dead already. And I didn't quite know how I'd handle that.

*******

# 21
## ❧Submerged❧

"Why take your grandfather, Ellie?" Jim asks as he signed off on the team's travel and dive orders. "Sorry to say, but he isn't monetarily or politically important. And the group I was with - well, they targeted vagrants and runaways – nothing too 'high profile', but also no one too challenging to get to. From what the girls said, it sounds like the men who took your grandfather tracked and targeted him; not exactly a target of opportunity".

Jim was right, but I knew this was different. "No Sir - and that is what worries me. I think they are trying to get to *me*". Forrest raised an eyebrow, so I explained, "I'm sending mom with the girls away and getting them off the radar. No trips to old family homes in New England, no long weekends with Aunt Chele in Mississippi. Nothing predictable. I can't risk my girls or any other members of my family".

"Where are you sending them?" Forrest asked, signing off on their protection order.

"Don't know yet," I answered honestly. "But you can be damn sure that no one will find out where they went until they get back".

\*\*\*\*\*\*\*\*

Having spent time with the 'less insane' group of travelling heretics, Michaels was able to almost confirm where he thought they were headed.

"Ellie, there was a LOT of talk; I'm just not really sure", Michaels said. "My group - they were a bunch of chatter boxes, always talking and gossiping". Before I could interject, he raised his hand slightly, and continued, "They talked about everything, but … it was *always* through a lens of their faith. You couldn't have a bowel movement without someone proclaiming it to be an act of the Lord". Aaron fell silent for a moment before he continued. "I heard a lot of things. I'd heard enough rumor and whispered conjecture to see that they were headed to the old sunken city of New Orleans, but I didn't know if I could trust that". Michaels stopped, and looked me straight in the eyes. "After a while, I didn't know what to trust. Every moment felt like a setup, like a trap. If you did the wrong thing... people just went away".

"Aaron, we have a lot of work to do". I placed a friendly hand on his shoulder. "Are you up to this?"

Aaron Michaels, a man I'd known since we were in high school, sat in silence for a moment. He knew I wanted an honest answer, so he stopped to ask himself, instead of giving a knee-jerk, pre-programmed response.

"New Orleans sank years ago, Ellie. There's nowhere to go. Are we missing something?"

"I think we are. Zim sent a drone. There is more there than we can see from here".

"What do you want to do?" Michaels asked. It was the first time in recent memory I could tell that he really didn't know what path to take.

"We have different paths, my friend. *You* go back to the Preterist. Re-integrate, and follow them".

I paused, reviewing the images we'd seen from the drone we sent to old New Orleans. *"We dive"*. I gave Michaels a strong hug. "We'll meet in the middle".

********

It took us three days to get everything in order. We covered everything from Zim's diving credentials to re-inserting Michaels into his group of Preterist. Regardless of all the details, in that short time we had Michaels headed back to the group we'd pulled him from, and Zimmerman and I were headed to dive deep in old New Orleans. It was dangerous, and we were acting on an unproven theory. But we were acting, and we'd know soon enough if we were right. The whole time, I kept worrying about my grandfather, and every time I let anyone around me know, I was reminded that they had taken him, not killed him outright. That fact alone usually meant he was being saved for a reason. If they wanted to control me, they could have killed him on the spot, leaving my girls as an open target, as a reason to comply. But he'd been taken; hostages were a completely different creature, from a psychological standpoint. So as much as I was afraid, until there was a demand, I knew he was safe. And that was their mistake. If he was safe, I could fight. And if I could fight, I could win.

\*\*\*\*\*\*\*\*

Michaels easily reincorporated with his group, just outside of Baton Rouge, Louisiana. They welcomed him with open arms, and hardly questioned his tale of release from the government penitentiary. As far as they knew, he'd gotten way from 'the man', and run off to find his brothers and sisters. In many ways, Aaron had the easier path in this. All we needed him to do was to follow the Preterist. Zimmerman and I.... we had a different task.

We entered the water on the south end of Lake Pontchartrain. Over the years, the size of the lake had grown, not only in depth, but in width. The southern edge now clawed its way down to the Mississippi River, completely enveloping not only the city that was once known as New Orleans, but much of the surrounding areas; suburbs like Metairie, Kenner and Chalmette, had all vanished under the water. Zimmerman and I took to our diving equipment and a couple of handheld transports to quickly move us across the distance, to get to the ruins of the Business District. Luckily for us, the drone we'd sent to review and observe had left us with something Michaels didn't have; we had coordinates, and a way to go directly to them.

While we were zipping along under the water, Michaels' group had finally reached their destination. On the western end of the lake, where the slope of the collapse was still evident above the water line, there was a collection of buildings that were just barely standing. One of them was an old Episcopalian Church. Once they entered the sanctuary, the Preterist led Michaels and the other 'new arrivals' back around behind the collapsed pulpit, and through a makeshift doorway. Michaels told me later that, in his head, he knew when they were below the water line, but the place had been carefully dug out, with the walls having been lined with sandbags near the entryway, and plaster and stone as they went deeper. After they'd gone another twenty feet, the tunnel hit another doorway, this one looking like it had once been the emergency exit of a school bus. As soon as they crossed the threshold, Michaels knew that was exactly what they were now in. The carefully dugout tunnel gave way to a string of busses, railroad cars and shipping containers that had been scrounged from God knows where. There was the occasional sound of a bilge pump, and Michaels knew then that wherever they were headed had electricity, and they were actively working to keep it warm and dry. It wasn't long before any sense of bearing or depths had been lost, leaving Michaels feeling lost as he followed the Preterist' down the poorly-lit passageway.

\*\*\*\*\*\*\*\*

Zim and I had a completely different vantage point. It was a good ten miles from the shore, and about three thousand feet deep where the drone had located the missing submarine. As fast as our underwater transport jets were, it still took us a half hour to get where we were going. We made the trip in silence, leaving each of us alone with our thoughts.

Once we hit the old Business District, it didn't take us long to find the partially-lit buildings the dive drone had locked in on. It was an eerie sight: tall buildings, lying at various angles and in various states of destruction, all collapsed in a pile, and all with a few windows here at there, lit well enough that, as I dared close in, and flipped down the digital binoculars that were built into my helmet, I could see living, breathing people going about their business in the ruins.

Only a short distance away, you could see where the massive columns supporting the raised platforms of 'new' New Orleans had been started. Even under hundreds of feet of water, with almost no sunlight trickling down to this level, you could still make out the massive supports, the broken platforms, and the collapsed buildings that had rested upon them. Barely a few hundred-thousand square feet of the Safeways had been constructed before Hurricane Joaquin not only flattened and flooded the city, but set off the underground firestorm that ultimately sunk the centuries-old city.

"Zim" I said over the comms. "Let's try to get to…"

Before I could continue, a series of spotlights came to life, sweeping across the general area we were diving in. I motioned to Zim to dive deeper, and we just avoided being caught by the searchlights. With that, it was time to go old school, and I pulled out my underwater marker and message flat from my side pocket. I swam up towards Zim, holding my hand in a 'STOP' motion, then writing on the message board, "No COMMS". He nodded in agreement as the lights made another sweep above us. After five or six of these passes, the search concluded, and the lights shut down. I wrote to him again, "Has to be triggered by radio waves; too much movement down here for motion sensors".

Zim gave me the thumbs up, and brought out his own emergency message flat, scrawling (in his ever-so-horrible handwriting), "where to now?"

I motioned for him to follow me, and we swam a little higher, back to a level where we could see the dark form of the submarine. I pointed to the

MURDERER'S SLAVE, and gave him a 'thumbs up'. My guess was, if we went in close enough to the body of the sub, we'd find a way in. It had to be docked somehow, and that gave us an opportunity. Zim, however, simply hung his head for a moment, shaking it back and forth.

It was great, knowing my team had faith in me.

## 22
### ❧Discovery❧

We quickly found out that entering the facility alongside the submarine was a no-go. From what we could see, it looked like the sub had been well moored, and was literally butted up against the wall of rubble. Since that didn't pan out, Zim and I scoured the general area, looking for any nook or cranny that we could use to enter. Our opportunity presented itself when Zim found access to an air pocket underneath one of the fallen buildings, and before we knew it, we'd shimmied our way through, and up into the hidden colony.

I took off my dive helmet, allowing it to fold back along the top of my air tanks. We each helped one another remove the heavy equipment, and set the tanks to start their auto-refill process. If we had to come back out this way, we'd have a full supply of air to get us home. If we found another way out, I was perfectly content to leave the equipment here.

"Looks like someone put a lot of work into making this place watertight," I said, placing my small hands against one of the stone walls. You could feel a small vibration running through the walls of the underwater structure. "Water pumps; probably salvaged from the old city".

Zim nodded, pulling out his handheld, and searching for technology. "Whatever it is, it's old enough to not be computerized. I'm reading the energy use, but no tech running it". Zim turned around a few times, then leveled his handheld against the wall. "Now, *here*, I'm reading tech".

I took a moment to get my bearings, and realized that Zimmerman was now pointed in the general direction of the submarine we'd been looking for. "Think we can get there from here, Zim?" I asked.

Zimmerman put on his best 'New Englander' accent, and said, "Nope; ya can't get there from here; ya gotta go 'round thattaway".

Making our way quietly through the lowest section of the sunken abode, we could occasionally grab a signal from Michaels. Between all the rubble, the metal and stone walls, and all the crap in the water, we were lucky to have an earful of static. So for the time being, I decided to sign out, and we'd try again later. It took us probably ten minutes to reach a junction that opened up into a larger space, and we quickly found some boxes to hide behind, just in case someone wandered too close.

"Ok, we're here" Zim remarked, looking around the ruined building we were now inside. "wherever 'here' is. As empty as this place is, we'll be lucky if it hooks up with any of the other infrastructure".

"I doubt they'd have dug out spaces just to leave them empty", I said, looking around the room. "Maybe this is an expansion or something, but it's got to hook up with the rest of the facility".

I took my handheld, and set it to record our trek, not only to map the area we were in, but to help us find our way out if needed. The place wasn't exactly what I'd call 'well-lit', and it would've been easy to get lost in the darkness. That was also a blessing, since our black dive suits helped us hide in the shadows.

"El, remind me *why* we are looking for the submarine, and not for Charles or your grandfather?"

"We don't really have any other place to start Zim," I answered quietly, pausing my conversation as a few people passed through an adjoining hallway ahead. After they passed, I continued, "Since the Preterist and the Pirates are working together, we might as well start with the one thing we know they both need".

"The sub," Zim answered back. "And the Preterist need the sub for…?"

"I thought of that ahead of time. If these really are the same folks responsible for the *Porcelain Death*, we know that it takes a radioactive source to activate the virus. And, we know the pirates are working with them; the sub they have is an old Oscar II class nuclear submarine from Russia. So that's their radiation source. And since they have that, we can use the sensors on our handhelds to find the submarine".

"And that helps us find your grandfather how?" Zim asked shyly.

"One step at a time, damn it", I answered, locking on to the submarines' nuclear core.

The directional sensor on my handheld said the source was about seven-hundred yards away, but that might as well have been a mile or more. In the ruined buildings, modified sewage ducts, and hand-dug tunnels, it was easy to get lost, and with all the twist and turns, it took us a while to navigate the poorly-lit passages once we hit the main cluster of buildings.

********

Michaels lost track of time as he followed the Preterist deeper under the ground. The passageway was dank and narrow, smelling of wet dirt and mold, but as they went further in, the number of lights started to increase, and eventually the tunnel opened up into a large, spacious place, that was not only well lit, but teaming with people.

"Welcome to our living quarters, brothers and sisters!" the head of the line announced. "Find yourself a spot, and enjoy all the community has to offer!"

The group Michaels had entered with began to break up, so he too started meandering about. The place looked like a third-world Bizarre, with people set up selling food, clothing, personal supplies, and much more. All the basic necessities were available here. There was even a man selling 'maps' of the old city, *'just in case you got lost'* among the ruins. Between the vendor booths, there were little camps of people scattered all about, sitting together talking, singing songs, and cooking food. It looked like a weird summer camp, and literally hundreds of people were participating.

As Michaels looked for an out of the way place to settle in, he wandered past another vendor, who was behind his table tinkering with something small in his hands. On the table were spread dozens of the creepy crucifixes we'd been finding, all apparently hand-made by the man behind the table.

"Blessings, son", the man said, looking up from his work. "May I help you?"

"Just window-shopping, sir," Michaels answered, picking up one of the larger Crucifixes. "Beautiful craftsmanship, my friend. Do you make them all?"

"I was given a gift, son. It would be a shame to not share it as intended". The man put down a newly completed piece on the table. "Yes, I make them all. No one topside wanted our business, so, we take care of it ourselves". He smiled, and waved his hands around, motioning to all the other vendors, "Just like we do with everything else".

Michaels laughed a little, looking around the room. Across the room, past the crowd, Michaels saw a familiar set of clothes moving toward a distant exit. It looked to be one of the Pirates, but at this distance, he couldn't be sure.

"Oh, there's my friend!" Michaels said to the jeweler. "Pardon me, sir". The man nodded and went back to his work, freeing Michaels to quickly cross the crowded room. Sure enough, as Michaels drew closer to the man, he could make out the same cut, the emblems, everything about the military style uniform that he'd seen too many times already. The pirate went down a back corridor, and Michaels, keeping his distance, covertly followed.

The 'living area' had been fairly nice, considering that is was hundreds of feet below the water, and built amid the ruins of buildings and broken soil. But every passage and corridor Michaels had seen so far looked like something from an old World War II documentary. Stone and brick walls, beset with pipes and tubes, barely dotted with lights seemed to be their chosen decorative style. As the pirate went lower into the bowels of the facility, Michaels found that the water pumps weren't working as well, and ended up having to quietly move through puddles here and there to keep up with his target. Ahead of him, Michaels heard the resounding echo of a metal door closing, and picked up his pace. Eventually, the corridor opened up into a larger area, with three passages leading away, and a closed set of doors off to one side.

Michaels started to creep toward the doorway when it started to open, so he quickly took a few steps back into the nearest corridor to hide in the shadows. The pirate he'd been following exited the room, leaving behind whatever package he's been carrying, and quickly jaunted back through another passageway. Giving him a moment to make sure he was gone, Michaels knelt, and crept back into the open area, and along the wall until he made it to the doors, which he slowly opened.

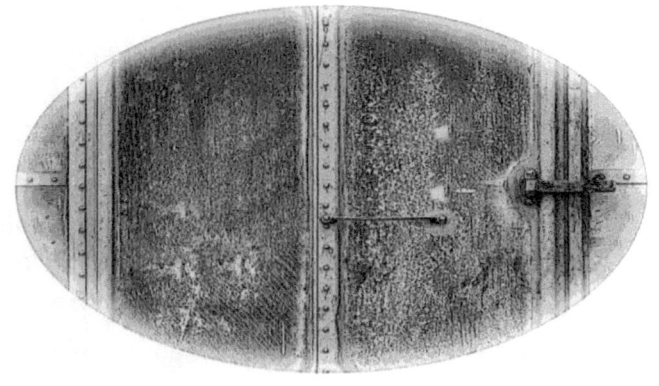

This room was well lit, and full of equipment, lab tables and medical devices. Michaels looked behind him to make sure it was clear, and stood up to slide quickly into the room. As he stood, he scanned the room for Preterist or Pirates, and saw none. But Michaels wasn't alone; sitting on the far side of the room, shackled to a raised desk, and dutifully plugging away at a computer terminal, sat Charles McFarlane.

## 23
### ❧Revealed❧

Since he'd seen the pirate leave the room, and saw no one else, Michaels' first impulse was to run toward Charles and free him. Charles' eyes widened as soon as he recognized Aaron across the room, but he quickly switched to a 'coughing fit', followed by a very subtle 'no' shake of the head. Michaels watched Charles' face as he motioned with his eyes to a camera just above the doorway. Had he stepped even a foot more into the room, Michaels would have been discovered.

His beard has grown out and he looked exhausted – but otherwise, Charles McFarlane looked alright from a distance. Seeing that helped Aaron control his built-in urge to free his 'friend', and

Aaron stepped back, grabbing his pulser from deep within the folds of the rags he'd been wearing as clothes. Turning a small knob on the side of the weapon, we switched it to 'taser' mode, and got just below the camera.

A small bolt of electricity shot forward from the front of the pulser, and found its target near the body of the security camera. A surge of electricity engulfed the video unit, and then it fell silent and still. The red operational LED had shut down, and its slight back and forth motion ceased.

Most people would have taken that as a sign that they were free and clear, but not Michaels. He lurked around the corners of the camera's field of vision, and finally found a broom and dustpan that was fairly close to the doorway. Grabbing the broom, Michaels got underneath the camera and knocked it to the floor. He dropped the broom, and turned to Charles McFarlane.

"It's about god-damn time you guys got here!" Charles said, holding up his shackles for Aaron to see. Aaron told me later that, despite the bravado Charles was displaying, he had tears welling up in his eyes. Aaron had finally gotten a chance to see something that I knew had been there all along, buried in the mass of ego, success, and failure to do more. It had been buried under his fear for years. It was his goodness; it's why Charles began to help us in the first place. And that good man, despite all his failings, hadn't deserved the hell he'd been put through.

Michaels finally moved closer to Charles, reaching into another hidden pocket for a set of lock picks (We may have been high tech, but you go in prepared; lock picks are a must). While Aaron worked on the locks of the shackles, he noticed that the edges of both of Charles' hands were bandaged.

"What happened here?" Michaels asked, trying to interact as he felt the turning of the tiny tumblers in the locks.

"I didn't cooperate," Charles answered, as one hand was freed. "My first few days in captivity, they gave me orders". Charles grabbed his left wrist as Michaels freed his other hand. "You know how I am".

"Ask, and you'll help," Michaels said, tossing the shackles aside.

"And tell me to do something?" Charles asked, sliding down from his workstation.

"You'll tell them to get stuffed", Aaron answered.

Charles nodded his head. "They didn't like that. So they cut off my right pinky the first day". He held up his left hand, adding, "And the left one the second".

Michaels gently grabbed Charles' left hand, and moved the bandages aside, to see a partially healed wound where his pinky finger should have been.

"So you cooperated?" Michaels asked, letting go of Charles.

"Not right then, no". Charles stopped and raised the sleeve of his dirty lab coat, revealing dozens of deep wounds, some healed into scars, others obviously recent. "I've done my best, but..." Charles dropped his sleeve, "they are persuasive".

Michaels lowered his head, feeling a bit shameful for having disliked Charles McFarlane so much, but something had changed in my old beau.

Charles reached out, placed his hand on Aaron's shoulder, 'til he looked up at him. "No, I didn't deserve it; no one ever would". With this, Charles got to his feet, straightened his back and shoulders, and looked to Michaels, saying, "Right, monkey?" adding a wink for good measure. Aaron saw exactly what Charles was reaching for, so he nodded, responding, "Yep; not even an ass like you!"

My boys were finally bonding.

********

They decided to not immediately leave the room. Michaels tried to raise me again on the comms, but only got a tiny bit of my message about looking for the submarine by the radiation signature. By now, Michaels had figured out that I'd hoped we could take the sub to get away from this place, which is why we'd gone in bare, with no additional dive suits or oxygen supplies.

While we were talking, Charlie was gathering all the data he could, and working to load it onto a small file drive. While they'd not truly trusted him, the Preterist had been forced to give him access to technology that they otherwise might not have shared. Charles loaded all his notes and research into

- 274 -

two flash drives, giving one to Aaron, and holding onto the second himself. As they worked, Charles updated Michaels on his story.

"They jumped me in my lab," Charles said, moving to another comm and hooking up the flash drives to download info.

"Sounded too familiar," Michaels answered, pulling actual 'paperwork' and folding it into the lining of his outfit.

"I hit one of them with a syringe full of my recreation of the virus; but they broke off his arm to keep the bastard alive," Charles said, scanning more data onto the drive.

"We found that; we weren't sure if it was yours," Michaels challenged, moving closer to Charles. "We only had one defining trait to go on, but…"

"That could have been removed, right?" Michaels didn't need to answer. Charles held out his right arm, and pulled up the sleeve, revealing a faded tattoo that read 'Ellyandra'. "I started to remove it," Charles started, answering the unasked question.

"Over the years, I chose to let it remind me of various things".

"Such as?" Michaels asked, in a somewhat defiant tone.

Charles looked at him for a moment, then answered, "Such as foolishness, loss, longing…" but before Michaels could respond, he continued, "then, over the years, as a reminder of lessons learned; of lost things found… of forgotten dreams".

They both went back to their work, but after a time, Aaron spoke up. "Laser treatment didn't take it off the first round, did it?"

Charles stopped cold. "Nope; I took that as something I should listen to".

Michaels and Charles worked for another ten minutes before either of them spoke again. Eventually, Michaels asked, "Any idea of what these bastards are up to, Mr. McFarlane?"

"More than I wish I knew," Charles answered. "I've been hearing their dogma for months. Since I was working on their 'cure', I heard it all".

"Cure?" Michaels asked. "What cure? Cure for what? The *Porcelain Death*?"

"No, Monkeyboy," Charles answered, holding a flash drive out to Michaels. "A cure for Humanity".

Michaels listened carefully as Charles told him what he knew about the Preterist. Their leader, Jeremiah Power, had been travelling the country, setting up little groups to preach their message, and lead his 'pilgrims' back to the holy city of New Orleans. His message was clear; most of Humanity needed to die. As extreme as that sounded, Michaels wasn't surprised to learn that thousands of disenfranchised people had heard this message, passed through a very loose filter of Christianity, and decided it was an act of faith to follow Jeremiah on his 'holy quest'.

"But Charles," Michaels asked after a while, "how could this group of people even get the tech needed to research something like the *Porcelain Death*?"

"Two points, Monkeyboy," Charles began, finally pulling the last of his data onto the second flash drive, and handing it to Michaels. "First, he may be a fanatical crackpot, but whatever else he is, Jeremiah Power isn't stupid".

"Did you call 'him' Monkeyboy, too?" Michaels asked.

"I wouldn't dare," Charles answered, adding, "That's your nickname. His nickname is dumbass".

"Did you say that to his face?" Michaels inquired.

Charles held up his left hand and pointed to the bandages where his pinky had been. "He may be intelligent, but he doesn't have much for a sense of humor".

Michaels nodded solemnly. "What's the second point, Charles?"

Charlie stopped, the faint smile briefly leaving his face, as he stared off into a memory. "A lot of smart people are desperate for belonging. Desperate people make deals with the devil, and say it was for the greater good". Charles shook his head a bit, and continued, "Remember how I said I'd seen the precursor to this virus in old man Waldorf's research?"

"Yeah, but how…?"

"They never told me how they got hold of it," Charles interrupted, "but math is one of my strong points. It's a simple equation, really. Take a group of religious fanatics landlocked in the States, add a rumor of a terrible disease that fits their idea of Death incarnate, and mix in a few pirates for hire".

"You have any proof, Charles?" Michaels asked.

"Only my eyes, Monkeyboy; only my eyes".

A rumbling out in the hallway startled both of them. Charles took his shackles and loosely placed them back on his wrists, motioning to Michaels to hide under one of the dozen or so desk in the room.

Michaels had barely gotten his large frame tucked away when one of the pirates entered the room. Charles sat back at his worktable, scrawling away on a pad of paper. Seeing that all was 'well', the pirate waved his gun around the room in one sweeping motion, pointed his free hand at Charles and, holding his fingers in the sign of a gun, made 'shooting' motions at Charles, before he turned to leave. This time, the metal door locked behind him.

"Charming hosts you have, Charles," Aaron said, once he felt he had an all-clear, crawling out from under the desk. "Any idea when their next check-in will be?"

Charles held his wrist, as though he were checking his pulse. "A little under fifteen minutes. We should be ready, so we can get out of here".

Michaels spent a few minutes trying to raise me or Zim on our commlinks, and had gotten just enough info through the static-y, garbled connection to hear we were headed to the old sub at the bottom of the structure. With the 'map' of the facility Michaels had picked up earlier, he felt he could lead Charles through the dark corridors, avoid people as needed, and get there pretty easily. Charles agreed, committing the map to memory, and handing it back to Michaels.

"So, what exactly did they have you working on?" Michaels asked, passing the few minutes they had left until the guard returned.

"They wanted the virus to be in a liquid form, without the radioactive catalyst".

"Didn't you have it in a liquid form before they took you from Mobile?" Michaels probed.

"Yeah, I'd gotten to that point by then, but I'd used the Fukushima protocols to induce the needed radioactivity".

"Why do they want a liquid? Seems like they were doing enough damage with their damned magic powder!"

"Not enough for their taste, monkeyboy". Charles stopped and counted in his head, adding, "Two more minutes". As he went back to the workstation, and 'reshackled' himself to the table, he continued. "They wanted it in a non-radioactive, liquid form, so they can 'spread their word' by polluting water supplies, cloud seeding, etc. and help fulfill the work of Death by bringing the only true redemption, the redemption of Death, to the world".

"One minute?" Michaels asked, seeing Charles nod in reply.

"I've had to listen to their dogmatic crap for months," Charles said, turning his pencil back to the pad of paper, "but fortunately I don't buy into it. A lot of people do though. He's got thousands of followers, and they've planned something big, starting right here in the USA and using the Dark Zones as a launching point. They were only waiting on me".

"What were they waiting on you for? What do you mean they 'were' waiting?"

At that moment, the door lock turned, clicking loudly, and the metal door opened slowly, creaking on its rusty hinges. Michaels had stood quietly waiting, and just as they'd hoped, the pirate walked slowly into the room, shutting the door without so much as a glance at the wall behind him.

The pirate looked around a bit, and then made a slashing motion across his throat toward Charles. Only this time, Charles raised his right hand, and made the sign for a gun, saying 'bang' at the pirate. It was right about that time that Michaels knocked the pirate out from behind, hitting the man hard on the base of his skull with his pulser.

Before tying him up, Charles removed the top layer of the pirates clothing and placed it over his own. He then took his tattered lab coat, and bound the pirates' mouth in a large gag, as Michaels used zip ties to bind the hands and feet.

"So," Michaels continued, handing Charles the small hat that finished the pirate outfit, "you were saying?"

"I was about to say that they were waiting on me, but I've stalled them as much as I could. Reverend Power's got his own people too, and they watch me like a hawk".

"So you're almost to a breakthrough? You think you can make the virus active without the catalyst?"

Charles let out a deep sigh. "Hell, I broke that code in my first week here, monkeyboy. I've spent the rest of the time trying to cover up, and stall their development while I worked on a 'real' cure. But with the level of oversight, and the number of tests they run daily – it's done".

Michaels face went pale. "What do you mean it's done?"

"They have their bioweapon," Charles acknowledged, grabbing the pirates gun, and opening the door. "And they are getting ready to use it en masse; to do what they think is the 'Work of the Lord'".

\*\*\*\*\*\*\*\*

## 24
### ❧Bounty❧

Zimmerman and I were having a bit less luck working our way towards the radiation signature that we hoped would be the MURDERER'S SLAVE. From what I'd seen of this place so far, it utterly amazed me that human beings could live like this. At least the Dark Zones had some airflow, and only flooded during storms. This place was like being buried alive, only with a little more wiggle room.

One good thing that I see looking back was that the lower levels had almost no one roaming around. We'd only had to halt our progress and hide a couple of times, and even then, the people who passed us were so focused on doing what they needed to do, and leaving, that we probably could have tapped them on the shoulder and said hello without them stopping to ask why we were there. Michaels tried reaching us one more time, but the connection was still horrible. I wasn't sure if he heard me tell him that we were headed to the submarine. I had no idea at the time who or what he'd discovered.

Somehow, in the twisting habitrail of tunnels, we ended up one level above the submarine, looking down from an observation area. This portion of the underwater edifice looked like it had been carved out from a tall building that had fallen on its side. Platforms had been built to change walls into floors, and add levels between walls. The original floor levels had been opened up to create a large space for the submarine to dock into. Its tower and part of its upper deck stuck out of the water, with literally hundreds of thick power cables running into the ship through a cargo hatch.

Looking below, there was a small wooden pier that had been built all along the side of the vessel, with a short gangplank that led to an open entry hatch. Only one of the pirates was guarding the submarine entrance, and he was facing the main corridor, completely ignoring the observation area.

He was also unaware of the wooden slats that had been nailed to the walls as a crude ladder, which made no sound as I snuck down them, allowing me to creep up behind the guard and drop him with a swift kick and a well-placed punch. Zim darted up the gangplank, and, seeing that we had an 'all-clear' in the entryway, I pulled the fallen pirate up and into the sub, only then taking the time to bind and gag him. We found a nearby storage locker, and stuffed the unconscious man inside.

The rounds of *'hide 'n seek'* I'd played with the girls had only added to my FBI training. I found myself thinking both like a knowledgeable, grown woman, as well as a five year old girl, while Zim and I searched the boat. We carefully made our way to the bridge. I remembered the layout from having been on board last summer, and it didn't take us long to reach our destination.

Zim found one of the nearby computer terminals and sat down to tinker. "Ellie," he called quietly, "This thing is running everything in some weird, Slavic dialect".

"That makes sense, Zim," I answered, scanning the panel on the central seat with my handheld, and waiting for it to come to life. "This was an old Russian submarine. But that's odd," I continued, as the handheld started bringing up the panel I was scanning. "The Captain's seat is displaying everything in Spanish".

"Slavic and Spanish?" Zim said aloud. "That *is* a weird mix".

I fiddled around on the control panel for a bit before I found what I was looking for. "Here we go, Zim!" I said, finding the logs for the ship. Can you start a download on this while I scan through?"

"Sure thing, El". Zim answered, pulling a cable from his terminal and plugging it into the console on the center seat. "This stuff is really old school, Ellie. Their systems aren't even networked together".

"I'll bet that if you asked nicely, Forrest might let you keep it for your collection," I said, skimming through the log files as my handheld scanned and translated them. "But I don't think this sub will fit in your cubicle".

Zim looked a little disappointed, so I threw in, "Well, maybe a terminal or two". He started smiling again, just as I found a mention of an old man in a log heading. I scrolled back up, and opened the full text, holding out the handheld so Zim and I could read it together.

*"Captain wants the old man alive for now, so we tossed him in the old first mates cabin. It smells like death and roach spray in there, but the bed is comfortable, and we can easily keep a guard on him, even when we leave the ship. Personally, I want to do the old coot in myself, for all the damage he did to me on Tuesday. Old and weak my ass!"*

"That has to be my grandfather, Zim," I quietly exclaimed, barely containing my excitement.

"Unless these guys specialize in kidnapping feisty old man, that's pretty likely," Zim said coyly, re-accessing his terminal for information. "Looks like the First Mate's bunk is on level three, aft section". He pointed down a hallway at the back of the room, "We can head that way, and down after the fourth junction, and try and come up behind them".

"Not 'we', Zim, just me". He started to protest, but I raised a hand, and added, "I can do this on my own. I need you to get as much from this system as you can while I'm gone".

"Ellie, even if you do find him there, just how are we going to get out of here with your grandfather, anyway?" Zim, stood, coming just close enough to reach out to touch my arm gently. "We don't even have an extra dive suit for Michaels, let alone another person".

I couldn't help but smile, feeling a small, somewhat evil looking grin develop on my face.

"Zim, have you ever considered learning how to pilot a submarine?"

********

I left Zim to grab as much data as he could, and see about the logistics of piloting the submarine out of this place. I hated not being there to watch his back, but Zim was almost as good at hiding in plain sight as my girls were. He was slim enough that he could probably have turned sideways and hidden behind a power pole, so I left him to his work, and went slowly down the corridor. I got past the first two junctions before I saw a guard moving ahead of me. I had stayed crouched down, and as soon as I saw him, I stopped movement, and held my breath. It didn't take me long to see that he was moving away from me, but the guard could turn around at any minute. I hadn't wanted to waste the charge in my pulser, but the only safe way to drop this guy was from a distance, so I took careful aim, and let the lightning fly.

That one hit drained my pulser by almost a third, but the guard fell and I easily disarmed and restrained him, ensuring his silence with a nice, hearty strip of duct tape. Low tech, perhaps; but it worked *very* well.

The next guard I ran into was a piece of cake. He'd fallen asleep against the wall, so I woke him just long enough to knock him out. A few more zip ties, another strip of duct tape and down I went to level four. I'd taken a look at the internal map Zim had pulled up, but like the old scenario maps on the video games I'd played growing up, they were incomplete when compared to actually moving through the environment. There were more pipes and electrical cable than you'd have thought for a submarine, and that made it hard to scan ahead of yourself.

When I reached the ladder to level four, I stuck my head down the shaft first, just to see what I could. I was glad I did, because not ten feet away from me was the back of a pirate who was guarding the door to the First Mates' cabin. I gently placed my shoes on the ladder, slowly working my way down as I watched the guard fidget around. As soon as I saw I had a clearing, I jumped down to the floor, hitting the guard with a pulser shock as he was turning around. I put my weapon away, zipped up another pirate, and opened the door to the poorly guarded room.

The portal-like doorway opened with a loud creak, and the musty smell of sea and rust came wafting out from the darkness of the low-lit living space. There was a locker built into the wall, a small table and chair, with a half-finished meal left behind, and at the end of the room, there was a single cot, with a small, dark figure lying on its back, gently snoozing.

Even in the gloom, I could see the shadow-painted features clearly enough to know that it was my grandfather. I walked up slowly, so as to not startle the old man, and knelt down at his side. 'Grandda-'' was all I got out before I lost all ability to speak. Granddad's right hand had suddenly clamped tightly around my throat, his fingers wrapping just around my windpipe. He sat up into the light, and just for a second, I thought I was going to die by his hand. It was only when he could clearly see my face in the light that he immediately let go, and threw his arms around me, barely containing his sobs of relief and joy.

"Ellie!" Granddaddy cried, holding me tighter. "How did you find me?" Before I could begin to answer, he pushed me back asking, "Are the girls alright? Are they safe?"

"Yes, sir. They're fine". I pulled him to me again, kissing him on the forehead like he'd always done to me when I was little. "We need to get out of here".

"Just where *is* here, honey?" He asked, getting to his feet. He stood, and buttoned his vest up, then added, "The bastards stole my hat".

"That's OK, Granddaddy. We're in New Orleans, in an old submarine".

"That explains the smell - on both counts". As we made our way out of the room, he kicked the fallen guard for good measure, sticking out his tongue as we passed.

On the walk back, I caught granddad up on what had happened with the girls, and how they'd helped us identify the pirates. He was as proud of them as I was, but mostly he was worried over the the effect this might have on them. We both knew the girls had been through hell in their short life, and neither of us wanted to add to that.

The bridge was still low-lit, but Zim and I worked, and let Granddad take a load off his feet by sitting in the Captain's seat. I handed him my pulser, and told him to 'shoot anything that moved'. He stood guard so Zim and I could talk.

"Alright, Zim; I'll go find Michaels, and then we can move this boat and get out of here".

"Oh, I could pilot it, Ellie. But," Zim looked defeated, "this old girl isn't going anywhere".

That obviously put a wrench in my plans. "Why not?"

"She's been permanently moored, El". Zim pulled up a schematic of the internal systems, and pointed out seven large, red marks, three on each side, and one on the bow. "She's locked down and welded in place at these points. If we fire up the engines and try to move, we'll either tear the ship apart, or the city above us" I shook my head, wondering why the pirates would have allowed their vessel to be scavenged like this.

"On top of that", Zim added, "the power systems down here are all running off her reactor. There are just too many integrated systems; if we try and pull away, we'll bring the whole she-bang down on top of us".

*******

## 25
### ❧Brimstone❧

We broke the news to my grandfather, who was still sitting in the center seat, pointing my pulser back and forth between the entrances to the bridge. He listened, never taking his eyes off the doorways, sitting in stoic silence.

After a moment, he looked up at me and said, "Well, love. This is your department, not mine". Granddad turned the weapon over in his hand, holding out the handle to me.

I reached out and took the pulser, and placed it back into my holster, nodding to my Grandfather, then turned to Zim and asked, "We heard anything else from Michaels?"

Granddad used to tell me that that I was either the luckiest person in the world when it came to timing, or I had some 'sixth sense' that impressed the hell out of him. No sooner than I had asked, we heard Michaels clearly over the commlink.

"Ellie? Zim?" Michaels asked in hushed tones. "We're just outside the sub".

"We?" I asked. "What 'we' are you talking about?"

"I must've cut out earlier, Ellie. I found Charles McFarlane," Michaels answered back.

I sat for a moment in silence, both relieved that he was alright, and ready to kick his behind for all the stress he'd put us all through. "Bring him up, Aaron; but" I paused, choosing my words carefully, "he's got some explaining to do".

I wasn't quite sure what I'd do when I saw Charles alive and well. Last glimpse we'd caught was of him being subdued and thrown in the back of a jeep in the Nevada desert. Now, while I had hoped that he and my grandfather would be held in the same place, I didn't know if I wanted to hug him, or slap him.

Just for the record, slapping him won out. At first, at least; then I briefly hugged him and Michaels, and looked back to Charles, who was rubbing his left cheek with his bandaged hand. "How the hell did you end up here Charlie?" I asked, but that was just the first in a long line of uninterrupted questions that went something like, "Did they take you in Mobile, or Nevada? How did you get that ident signal out? What did you do with the stuff from Yucca Mountain? Do you know their plans? How do we get out of here? And just WHAT did you do to your hand?"

'Finished, Ellie?" Charles asked. "Because I've already told Monkeyboy here all those answers, but yea, since you finally noticed," Charles pulled back the bandage on his hand and showed me the wound. "They were insistent that I helped them. I didn't want to".

Suddenly, I wasn't the least bit angry or irritated with him anymore. "I see that went about as well as I'd expect".

Charles held up his right hand. "Twice. You don't want to see my arms".

********

It didn't take us long to think of a way out. Since we couldn't move the submarine without risking our lives, and we didn't have enough dive gear for all of us, there was only one way out. We'd have to go right back the way Michaels came in, right through the belly of the beast.

Disguises were the easy part. With all the pirates we'd captured, there were plenty of pirate uniforms for all of us. Michaels chose to keep the rags he'd come in wearing. If anyone recognized him, that would lend validity to the group of us. Also, Michaels had the map, so we'd have a much easier way out than we'd had coming in. The group quietly made its way up and through the passageways, towards the living quarters, but as they went, they came across more and more people.

"The Preterist aren't really interacting with us, are they?" I asked Michaels, straightening the militaristic jacket I'd stolen.

"Seems odd, Ellie. Everyone I met earlier was talkative and outgoing".

We walked through another fifty feet of a corridor before we hit the large, open area. Just like Michaels had described, it was huge, busy, and bristling with people. Michaels led us back to the place where he'd entered the room, but we found the entranceway was blocked by no less than six guards, and stacks upon stacks of small, white boxes.

"Oh, no," Charles said. "No, no no...."

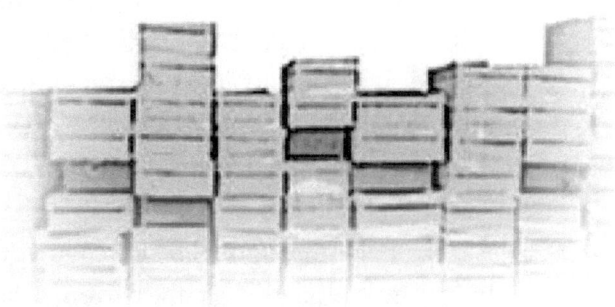

Michaels walked up to the guards, inquiring about passage back to the surface. He smiled quietly to the guards, and returned to us, saying, "Not yet; soon enough".

"What the hell does that mean?" Granddad asked, taking a seat on a nearby crate.

"I'm not sure, sir" Michaels answered. But until that time comes, they are too well armed for us to get past them".

We meandered close to the exit, pondering our next move. While Zim and Michaels talked quietly, I checked on my grandfather, then checked on Charles.

"No what, Charlie?" I asked. "I know that face; what did you do?"

He pointed to the stacks of white boxes. "I did what they made me do, Ellie". He then reached into his pocket and handed me a small flash drive, which I put away immediately. "I also did what they didn't want me to do, but... you'll need a sample".

With this, Charles removed the bandages on his left hand, and slammed the wounded corner against the nearby crate. I could see that he *almost* passed out from the pain, and blood started pouring down the crate, his arm, and onto the ground. I reached over to help, but he held up his right hand, then used his lab coat to wrap up the wounded appendage. After a few moments, he rewrapped his hand, then, in obvious agony, tore off part of the bloodied lab coat. This he wrapped tightly upon itself, and handed it to me.

"This goes with the data on the drive," Charles said, looking pale. It was only as he handed me the bloody fabric, that I noticed it had stiffened a bit.

"Charles Randolph McFarlane, what did you do?' I asked, afraid to hear the answer.

A loud gong unexpectedly sounded in the room, and everyone but the guards started moving towards the center of the living quarters. The middle of the large room was left empty. I looked over to Michaels, and both he and Zim nodded, with Zim reaching over to help my grandfather to his feet. We kept back, letting the real Preterist get close to the podium that we could barely see rising from the platform in the center of the room. A tall, thin man rode the platform up from below, and as soon as the motion stopped, a large, blue hologram of the speaker was projected thirty feet high, almost touching the ceiling.

"Jeremiah Power," Charles said quietly, looking at the hologram that was actively scanning the man, and projecting him larger than life for the crowd. "Get ready for a show, everyone".

We huddled close together on the edge of the crowd, holding back so we could listen.

"For an underground mudhole, they have a lot of tech," Zim observed, as spotlights started crossing back and forth across the ceiling.

"They've been salvaging as they dug out New Orleans," Charles whispered. "What they have is mostly old tech, or stolen items. But with that submarine, they've got all the power the need".

It was at this point that the crowd started chanting, "Power! Power! Power!" over and over, and the holographic figure that dominated the room smiled brightly, waving his hands in a downward motion to 'quiet' the crowd. Anyone who wasn't completely brainwashed by the man could easily see that he was eating up the attention and energy of the crowd.

As 'Reverend' Power placed his hands on the podium, the crowd fell silent. Charles leaned down and whispered in my ear, saying "Now you'll really see why this guy took the name 'Power'".

"My Children! My loving, brilliant survivors!" Power began, the hologram above him following every subtle motion of his face and body. "Today, we begin a task that has been over two millennia in the making!" The crowd roared its approval, then fell silent again with the raising of Power's hand. "By now, you ALL know what we face. You ALL know that we have been chosen to help the Servants of our Lord fulfill their roles, and to do so, we must all revel in the glory and bounty of our servitude!"

Charles couldn't hear me as I covertly commented, "This guy is a nutcase". I didn't notice at the time that, while Charles hadn't heard me, one person did. One person, who'd been circling the perimeter of the crowd, and who darted away into the dark behind us after hearing me.

Power continued, gently wooing his already smitten crowd. "Today, my children, the Spirit of Death himself has spoken to me, and he has brought his glorious work to US, to his CHOSEN, to fulfill the last of the Great Book!"

The crowd cheered again, spellbound by the speaker. I thought back to what the archbishop had told me. He'd said, *'They are con artist, madmen, and terrorist. They are everything vile and unjust; but they sure as Hell aren't Christian'.* The more I listened to this man, who projected his image larger than life above the crowd, the more I understood just how right the Archbishop had been.

"Today, my children," Power continued, "Today I send you out into the diseased world around us. I send you into the Lake of Fire, but you will not burn! You will be doing God's work, and you will prevail!"

With this, Jeremiah Power held up one of the white boxes we'd seen stacked by the hundreds by the exit. "Here, my children, I give you our key! Our Answer! Our OWN REVELATION!"

This time, the cheers of the crowd actually hurt my ears, and the reverberation of the sound created a visible disturbance in the holo emitter, causing the image of Jeremiah Power to shake and shimmy as it smiled, almost manically, looking down on the crowd.

"Now, my children, as we've trained, as we've gone through over and over; now -" Power held the box high above his head, and the holo image bent across the ceiling, "now TAKE UP YOUR ARMS! Do what MUST BE DONE!"

With this command, the Ultra-Preterist started moving towards the exit we'd been trying to reach all along, but now the guards were moving aside. Each of the people who marched by picked up one of the boxes, and went up through the dark corridor that led to the surface. Reverend Power continued to talk as they marched along.

"You go on to greatness! You will DO what MUST be DONE! And in the sin you commit, in the Name of the Lord, and His Servants, you will be redeemed! You will have LIFE ETERNAL!"

The roar of the crowd was almost unbearable, and our little group hung back as best as we could, lest we find ourselves swept into the moving tide that was flooding towards the exit. The Preterist were moving as one mind, one body, and with one purpose. They intended to use whatever was in those boxes to kill as many people as they could.

I pulled Charles close to me, more roughly than I'd wanted, considering his injuries. Bringing his ear close enough to ensure he could hear me, I asked him point blank, "Charlie, what is in the damn boxes?"

He looked me in the eyes, gently taking my face in his right hand, and turned my head so his mouth was directly above my ear. "It's Death, Ellie. Death they forced me to make".

I moved away, to look Charlie in the eyes, but he had nothing more to tell. He'd given us the details in both research, data files, and literally in blood. He looked at me, and just shook his head, as though he never really believed it would happen.

But it had already happened; it was happening right then, right now, right in front of us, right in front of our eyes; it would keep going, on and on, regardless of what we could do. And no amount of disbelief would change that.

********

The Preterist kept up the energy for a good half an hour, which was, despite the number of people they had to serve; long enough to pass out most of the stacks of white boxes that Charles had said were filled with 'Death'. We kept ourselves shuffled to the back of the line, so no matter how close we got, we hung back and let others go ahead.

Maybe things would have been different, if we'd just gone ahead. But I could second guess myself for several lifetimes, and never truly know.

Finally, almost no one was left ahead of us, so hanging back would have been a problem. Even Jeremiah Power himself had come down from his pulpit, taken a white box, and led a group of followers to the surface. So, there we were, dressed in the garb of the pirates, and surrounded by, of all people, the pirates that had been hired not only as muscle, but servants as well.

Michaels stepped up to the front of the line, and took the white box they held out to him, nodding ecstatically as we'd expected he should. As soon as he moved to the opening of the corridor that led to the surface, he hung back in the shadows, waiting. Zim moved through next, catching a raised eyebrow from the pirate who was passing out the boxes, but he too was handed one of the containers, and allowed to pass.

Then, it was my turn.

Do you remember me saying that 'fate was a fickle friend', all those years ago? Well, fickle friends don't always have your back, and as I approached the pirate to receive my package, another pirate, more elaborately dressed, walked out of the shadows, right past me, and bent over to whisper in the ear of the man who was passing out the white boxes.

When you are trying to covertly move through the enemy lines, pauses are never a good thing. They give fate opportunities to screw you over. Always beware the unplanned pause.

When the new pirate stood back up, and turned, I could swear that I knew his face. I tried to hide my own visage, just for safety sake, but something about him reminded me... of a man I'd worked with in the Dark Zone in Miami last year.

"Sergeant Tiermo," I said quietly to myself, almost absent-mindedly.

The man stopped, and turned to face me.

"I haven't been called a mere 'sergeant' since," …

It was at that moment that Tiermo saw my face. I didn't know then that mine was a face he'd looked at night after night for months, as he screamed, cried, fought, and plotted his revenge. Last I'd seen, he was leading a few rag-tag pirates out of the auction house in Miami. Now, he was here, staring me in the eyes, with a murderous look giving away his intent.

"YOU!" Tiermo cried. "I am going to KILL you!"

Maybe I was raised in a weird decade, but, looking back on it, I remember the fight as being like something out of a video game. Michaels and Zimmerman immediately returned from the open passage, and Charles gently pushed my grandfather behind him, even though he knew he couldn't really fight in his condition.

Oddly, the remaining guards stepped back as well, as though they'd been prepared for this possibility, and been given orders long before we ever entered the sunken city.

Michaels and Zimmerman both engaged the guards at the tunnel's entrance. Hand to hand turned into wrestling, then outright brawling. Zim landed a solid punch on the jawbone of one of the pirate guards, knocking the man out cold. Of course, Zimmerman almost broke his right hand doing so, but he told me later that he was just glad to help.

Michaels stood up to the second guard, who'd brandished a knife for their battle. But at the time, I had to focus on Tiermo, who stood in front of me like a statue, readying his attack with all the hatred and bile he had built up for me.

The next few minutes are still a blur to me. I lashed out in a defensive stance; Tiermo countered, punching through my defense. It went on and on, move after move, each of us landing hits on one another that would have incapacitated anyone else. It was only our level of training that kept us standing, and able to fight on.

I'd never fault my grandfather for wanting to do what he thought could be his part. But, if granddad hadn't jumped in, Tiermo may not have found the leverage he needed. My grandfather plunged into the fray, hitting and clawing as best as he could against the man who'd been attacking me, but Tiermo was too strong. Granddad found himself overpowered by the younger and stronger man, who took my grandfather in his hands, and, bringing the old man down across his own limbs, broke Granddaddy's' right leg with an audible crack.

Granddad screamed out in pain, as he was literally tossed down like a ragdoll. Instincts kicked in, and I stopped my counter-attack to cautiously head to my grandfather's side. As simple as that human act seems, it gave Tiermo the advantage he'd been looking for.

Pulling a hand-cannon from his coat pocket, Tiermo leveled the sights at my head. My attention was elsewhere, trying to get my grandfather's eyes to focus through his pain. I looked back at Tiermo, who was leveling his weapon at me, and screamed, "You sorry son of a bitch! What the HELL is WRONG with you?!"

My defiant tone didn't sit well with my executioner, but at that moment, I didn't care. Granddad had passed out, and I laid his head gently on the ground. Afterwards, as the fire burned in my chest, I turned toward the man who'd hurt my grandfather, with hate glowing in my eyes.

"I'm going to kill you," I said to him, softly, unemotionally.

"I have the gun, fool", Tiermo answered, cocking the hammer and solidifying his aim at my head.

"Then do it, you piece of shit!" I growled, starting a slow, steady approach. 'This is the only chance you'll have, so DO IT NOW!"

You know how people will tell you that, in the most fearful, or horrible moments of their life, time seemed to slow down for them? I'd heard that all my life, and occasionally experienced it to some degree. But, as I approached Tiermo, seeing Michaels and Zim finally overcoming the men they'd been fighting, time didn't slow. If anything, it skipped. Time skipped along, missing precious milliseconds, jumping over heartbeats, and, despite the unbroken narrative that time tells, missing the opportunity to stop what was happening.

I approached Tiermo; I saw him pull the trigger.

I saw Charles come out of nowhere, and jump in between the quickly moving bullet, and its original target. I saw his neck almost explode in a flurry of blood, and I saw the tiny pieces of his flesh that flew around in a sphere, some hitting me, some landing on Michaels and Zim. And through it all, as I watched Charles McFarlane fall into a wounded, bloody heap in front of me, I heard Tiermo laughing.

Even after the echo of the gunshot died in the cavernous room, I still heard Tiermo laughing.

Charles fell backwards, almost right into my arms. I moved to catch him, and tried in vain to grab the gushing wound on his neck. Holding my friend, I knelt to give his body a spot to rest on, as I tried futilely to apply the pressure needed to keep him from bleeding out.

Tiermo looked over to my now broken grandfather, then across to Michaels and Zim, who looked ready to pounce him. Re-aiming his gun at my head, he asked, "Children, you really think that's a good idea?" My boys exchanged a look. Tiermo again cocked the hammer of his gun. "Nah; just drop it, kids. Drop it, or she dies right now".

Michaels and Zimmerman both backed down; Zim moved fast and low towards my grandfather, to see what kind of care could be given. Michaels did what I knew he'd do; he moved close to me, almost behind me, just waiting for a word from me to strike.

Tiermo looked down on Charles, who was still bleeding out in my arms. As much as I tried, I couldn't keep the blood from flowing. My hands simply weren't enough to make a difference. I looked up at Tiermo, and said again, "I *am* going to kill you".

I said it slowly, without malice. It wasn't a threat; I was stating a fact. I was going to kill this bastard and be damned the consequences.

"I don't think you'll have the chance," Tiermo responded, waving the gun in a motion to move us away from the door. The guards, got to their feet, and placed two small, metal boxes on the entryway of the tunnel that lead out, then walked away into the dark corridor toward the surface.

Tiermo backed himself up to the exit, and, using his free hand, pulled a strange-looking comm unit from his coat pocket.

"This," Tiermo said, "this is your doom; so watch your fool die in your arms. You all die with him!" With this, Tiermo pushed a control on his comm, and the entire facility started to shake. "With this, you all die".

Zimmerman called out, "El, he's activated his submarine!"

Michaels struggled in the shaking edifice to keep his footing, and go after Tiermo, but the man was too quick. As soon as the Pirate had passed through the doorway, the tiny explosives that had been planted went off, collapsing the entrance of the tunnel, and trapping us all in the living quarters that would soon themselves collapse on top of the now-moving submarine.

And throughout all this, my grandfather lay unconscious, wounded and broken, and my former fiancée lay in my lap, bleeding to death from a wound I knew could never be healed in time to save him.

## 26
### ❧Loss❧

As soon as Tiermo had gone through, and the tunnel opening collapsed, Zim pulled his handheld out of his pocket, and started plugging in commands.

"I'm still tied into the sub's computer, El," Zim cried out. "I think I can, YES!" He almost screamed as he shut down the submarine's engines, and the shaking stopped.

I still sat with Charles in my lap, drenched in his blood. "Zim," I said quietly. "Will you please look after granddad?" Zim nodded and moved to my grandfather's side, trying to gently rouse him.

"Aaron," I continued, looking down at Charles' face. "Will you please see if we can dig out that entryway? Otherwise, we'll need another way out".

"You got it, Ellie," Michaels answered, turning immediately to the work at hand.

They both already knew what I didn't want to admit.

I turned my attention back to Charles, gently caressing his face. "Alright Charlie, cut out this nonsense, hon". It reminded me of *his* kind words two years ago, when he saved my live in the Dark Zone in Mobile. We weren't in love anymore; hadn't been for years. But, as a wise person once said, *"You never fully fall out of love, if you were ever really in love to begin with"*.

"You're going to be alright, Charles. Just... just hold on".

I knew I said it, but I wished I had believed it. Charles struggled to talk a little, but all that came out of his mouth was a flood of blood, bubbling and frothing as he tried to breathe. I looked more closely at the wound; his speech box was gone, as was half his throat. I looked around, my training kicking in. At least five pints had already spilled out. There was just too much damage, and quite frankly, I was surprised that he was still hanging on.

"Ellie!" Michaels cried, bringing my attention to him. "The damage was superficial. Just a few feet of mud and dirt to dig through, and we're out!"

"Keep going Aaron! We need to get Charles help!"

As I said this, Charles reached up with what little strength he had, and grabbed me by the back of the head, crunching my hair in his hands, and bringing my gaze back to him. His eyes were wide opened, as he stared into mine.

In that moment, everything else around me stopped moving. I looked into his eyes, as more blood bubbled up from his mouth, and he firmly grasped the hair on the back of my head.

The moment had come.

I tried to not let tears take control, and I grabbed Charles' hand from the back of my head, and took it into both of mine. "It's OK, Charlie," I said, reaching out to touch his face through the blood and tears. "It's OK Charlie. You can go, hon".

More tears welled up in Charles' eyes, and he grasped my hand just a little more tightly.

"Don't be afraid, hon. Shhhh" I said , brushing his hair aside. "You changed the world, hon. You changed me," I said, seeing his eyes unfocus.

"Sleep, my friend," I said, as the last of the blood poured from his wound. His eyes, while opened, went blank and empty. I reached over to close them, saying only, "Sleep, love".

The rest, as they say, was silence.

********

It took the FBI Special Ops unit three days to reach the sub through all the damage that had been done in its brief attempt to flee. We'd taken granddad, and the body of Charles, to the surface, and met Forrest there. It was a flurry of action, support, kindness... and loss. It took my grandfather several hours to regain consciousness, but as much as that hurt me, I still found myself lingering near Charles. When they took him away, I felt like I had when Roberts had died. I felt like a piece of me had been taken. It wasn't missing. It was just... gone.

Granddaddy went in for care at Mobile Memorial Medical Center, and the boys and I tried to regroup in the Federal Building to refocus, in hopes of gathering our strength and stopping what we knew was coming.

Aaron and Zim set up all the data from Charles' notes for reproduction in the holorecreator. Charles had implied that he'd created a cure, and we needed that above all else. If we could decipher it all there, and make sense of it, we might have a chance to stop the Preterist from carrying out their plan. Of course, we still weren't clear on what that plan was, so we decided we'd better be ready for anything.

Zim set up the holo-lab, and then went off to peruse the files and logs from the MURDERER'S SLAVE. Michaels and I worked to decipher Charles notes and formulas, but after only a few hours of work, it became evident that we were missing something.

Aaron pointed at a 'progress line' on the simulated screen. "Ellie, we're just hitting a wall".

I looked at the data myself, and nodded. "Charles said that we'd need something more".

I thought back, realizing that Charles, at great pain to himself, had given us exactly what we needed. "Aaron, pull up the scan we have of the bloody bandage that Charles gave me in New Orleans".

It took the computer fifteen minutes to render the sample at a molecular level. In our eyes, the holorecreator simply reconstructed the folded, bloodied piece of cloth that Charles had given me. But, to the computer system, when the sample was paired with the notes we had gotten from Charles, the two pieces of data fit together seamlessly. Between Charles' notes, and the blood sample he'd given us, we easily could see what he'd done. The work was, as expected, absolutely brilliant. But as good as it was, the cure had come with a huge price. Had Charles been working in a full lab, with all his resources, he'd not been forced to make the choice he'd had to make.

Charles had used his own body as a crucible for testing the retroviral for the *Porcelain Death*.

He was damn lucky that it had worked, or he would have been dead weeks before we reached him. And we were damn lucky that it had worked, or we wouldn't have had a clue how to reproduce the retroviral. Essentially, Charles fought to make sure he survived long enough for the cure to reach responsible hands.

********

While Michaels and I set the full force of the Government behind reproducing the cure en masse, Zim had fulfilled another task.

When we were in Old New Orleans, Zim had created an uplink to the submarines computer systems when he discovered that the sub was immobile. That uplink used the built in network in the Preterist hidey hole and stayed connected to Zim's handheld. That simple fact is what saved us all from being buried and/or drowned in the sunken city. But even after the sub was stopped, Zim still had full access to its computer.

And *that* fact is what made Zim call us all into a meeting. Of course, we met in my office. I had a coffee machine.

Forrest arrived first, securing his place in the only comfortable chair aside from my own. Michaels came in next, finding his usual spot alongside my desk, followed by Zim, who perched himself in his usual perch on the shelf by the coffee maker.

"Alright, Zimmerman," Forrest began. "You were awfully excited about this. Are you sure this doesn't have to do with some computer code that we'd need implants to even decipher?"

"Not at all, Sir!" Zim answered, hitting a few buttons on his handheld and passing the data over to the holo-link on my desk.

I looked over at Forrest. He looked just as he always had; strong, secure... normal. And while I may have known differently, I would never challenge him in front of anyone. That wouldn't help him, and it wouldn't help us.

"Alright, Zim," I said, plopping myself into my seat behind the desk, and putting my feet up. "What do you have for us?"

"I've got a timeline, Ellie," Zim answered, surprising us all. "And, I can prove it".

"Ok, Zimmerman," Forrest answered, leaning forward in his seat. "Enlighten us".

Zim looked quite proud as he spoke. I knew he'd been working hard on decrypting and analyzing the data from the computers in the MURDERER'S SLAVE, but I'd had no idea how much intel they'd given us.

"Well, the first thing I can clear up is, Galeno Tiermo had ordered the Pirates' foray into your apartment, as well as the 'peeping toms' you'd been dealing with".

We looked back and forth between each other; that didn't really matter in the grand scheme of things. Not at that moment.

"I can also tell you that when the MURDERER'S SLAVE was spotted in Oslo, late last year, they were under contract with Jeremiah Power".

"Wait a minute," Forrest started, "how can you prove that?"

"I found the contract entered into the sub's computer. They were sent to Oslo to retrieve shipping records from the Interpol bust two years ago on Reginald Waldorf's seized property".

Forrest sat in silence, though Zim had hoped for a reaction. After a moment, Forrest simply answered, "Continue, please".

"Well, there are a LOT of log entries, but only a few from the captain that held control before Tiermo".

"How the hell did a former Sergeant in Miami end up involved with a bunch of Pirates anyway?" Michaels asked. In response, Zim just looked at me.

"We... *I*... forced him there", I answered. "He and Director Cano had a sweet deal, working with the criminals in the Miami Zone; we broke the back on that whole operation".

"No one forced him, Ellyandra," Forest interjected, but I continued.

"No sir; but, we swept the rug from underneath him; the Pirates were there; it all just fell into place for him, I'd guess. Right, Zim?"

"Right, El; his logs show that's how he saw it, at least. And when they got the contract from Jeremiah Power," Zim said, pausing for us to fill in the details.

"They took the job, but Tiermo used the whole situation as an outlet for his revenge?" Michaels asked.

"Looks that way. The log entries are full of disparate, mad rants after Tiermo took control".

"How did the crew not notice?" I asked, looking over the data on my handheld.

"All his logs were in Spanish; the rest of the crew spoke Czech".

"They had no idea how mad he was, did they?"

Zim shook his head again."There's no evidence that any of the crew spoke Spanish; but we know from Federal records that Tiermo spoke three languages; English, Spanish, and Czech. He'd been trained in one of the 'eastern front' scares we had about ten years ago".

"Or fifty years ago," Forrest interjected, "or seventy, or a hundred. It's a cat and mouse game that keeps coming up, isn't it Zimmerman?"

"Sadly, yes sir; it's an old theme, with new players. Now," Zim pointed to a holo map he'd projected for us all, "Now it's everywhere".

The routes Zim had projected for the MURDERER'S SLAVE alone had taken it across the globe at least six times in one year. "There are fifty-six missing nuclear submarines from this era; twenty-two American, and thirty-four of what they used to call 'soviet' sourced".

"Right now, Zimmerman," Forrest said, stopping Zim's presentation, "we have the *one* sub we were worried about, am I right?'

"Yes Sir," Zim answered quietly.

"So we will have to worry about the rest later; what can you tell me about the people connected with *this* submarine?"

"Well, sir, I was getting to that; I just wanted you to have an understanding of…"

"Zim!" Forrest said loudly, quickly regaining his composure. "I see your point; so give us more. What else have you found?"

Zimmerman shuffled uncomfortably, but refocused himself so he could continue. "Well, sir, we know that the Preterist were actively using the virus to lead their 'pilgrims' to New Orleans".

"Old news, Zimmerman", Forrest responded, knowing that Zim had uncovered more info.

"According to the logs in the submarine, it looks like the Preterist were planning on injecting the virus into the water systems of each major town in the US. But they didn't say how".

I started tapping commands into my handheld, only to find that Forrest was already issuing the same commands.

"Think you could have told us this sooner, Zim?" I asked sarcastically.

"Maybe, but it's useless unless we have targets, El, and there were no specific targets given". Zim shifted his bottom on my bookcase, then added, "That's all I've got Ellie; that's all I've got right up until this meeting started".

"Then we've got a LOT of work to do", I said, looking solemnly at a map of the US. "How much ground could they cover in three days?

The answer was 'too much'. And we'd see that all too clearly, far too soon.

# 27
## ⊰Lockdown⊱

Forrest had gotten approval from Homeland Security to lead the task force to stop the Preterist, and had ordered National Guard teams to secure and protect the water treatment facilities at almost eight-hundred sites. It was an unprecedented level of protection, so when reports started coming in of a 'mutated' version of the Porcelain Death showing up in people in Texas, Arkansas, Mississippi and Tennessee, we were all scratching our heads as to how they'd gotten the new, non-radioactive version of the virus, into the water supply to begin with.

Of course, the media had done its part to completely freak out the general population. All it took was one reporter in Bellevue, TX to start the rumors of a 'pandemic', and before you knew it, there were runs on banks, near riots for food and supplies, and even a partial shutdown on the business sector, because people were literally hiding in their houses. All the military protecting the water treatment facilities only served to give rise to even more conspiracy theories, and led to more than a handful of clashes between National Guard members and the public. And all the while, despite riots, looting and chaos, people were still drinking their tap-water, and people were still contracting the *Porcelain Death*.

I left Zim and Michaels to run more simulations, and headed out to check on my grandfather. Granddad was laid up at Mobile Memorial, having had surgery to fix the broken leg he'd been given in New Orleans. It broke my heart to see the old man stuck in a hospital bed again, but his demeanor was *very* different than it had been before. I found my grandfather sitting up, flipping channels on the television in the room, looking dour each time the station landed on any news reports.

"Hello, my love," Granddad said as I entered the room. He motioned towards the screen, saying, "These damned idiots don't have a clue, do they?"

"No sir, they really don't," I answered, kissing him on his forehead and sitting down next to the bed. "How's the leg?"

"You remember an old TV show called the 'six-million dollar man?" he asked in response. I shook my head no. "Not surprised. It was on when I was little". He put down the remote control, and grabbed a display page from his bedside. On it was a growing list of charges, tallying each moment he stayed in the hospital. "I'm starting to feel like *this* is going to be six million, they way these leeches charge people".

"When are they going to release you?"

"Hell if I know, Ellie". Granddad shifted in the bed. "They spliced the rod to my leg, and gave me a nerve block on one side to ease the pain, and a nerve-enhancement patch on the other, so I can move more 'normally'; at my age, I haven't moved 'normally' in at least fifteen years".

I scanned down the page, and noticed a charge labeled 'scar tissue necroses. "What's scar tissue necroses, granddad?"

"If memory serves, its twenty three thousand, three hundred dollars," he answered straight faced.

"No, what does it *do*?" I replied, giving a slight chuckle.

"Only thing they could tell me was, that when they were doing surgery on my leg, they ran across some scar tissue from an old surgery that was in the way. Instead of cutting it off like anyone with any damn sense, they stopped the blood flow to that area, killing the scar tissue".

"Seems like a waste to me".

"You think that's bad?" Granddad got a mischievous smile on his face, and reached for the nurse's station call button. "Watch the bottom of the page". With that, he pressed the button, and a new charge line appeared on the bottom of the bill. *'One on one nursing consult'*. The charge sat at zero dollars for a moment, but kicked in just as the nurse opened the door.

"Yes, Mr. Dyett?" the pleasant woman asked. "What can I do for you?"

"Can I go home yet, miss?" my grandfather asked.

The nurse pulled up a tablet, and scrolled through a bit. "Looks like three o'clock today, sir. Is there anything else?"

"No, thank you hon," granddad answered. As soon as the door closed behind her, the charge stopped tallying.

"Well, at least that's good news" granddad said. "Now, how much was that, Ellie?"

"This says fifty-three dollars and sixty two cents".

"It triples if you need help going to the loo".

Granddaddy and I just looked at each other for a silent moment, then both burst into laughter.

********

By the time I got back to the Federal Building, I could see that something had changed while I was away. Sure, there were usually bunches of people going about their business, but this was more akin to a mound of ants, or an agitated hive of bees, than anything I'd seen before. I was nearly knocked over by a SWAT team that blew through the crowd on their way to a waiting transport, and the dull roar of the crowd echoed throughout each floor the lift stopped on.

I bounced into my office, shutting the door behind me, only to see Michaels and Zimmerman in their customary places, having already brewed a fresh cup of coffee for me. Zim turned my chair out so I could sit.

"If it's that bad guys," I said, sitting down and grabbing the coffee, "maybe this should be wine instead".

"Trust me, El, you'll need the coffee," Zim answered, moving into the seat Forrest usually took.

"I'm thinking with all the hubbub I had to fight to even get to my office, you and Michaels found something, yes?"

"We knew they were using the water supplies, right?" Michaels asked, reaching over to y desk and hitting a few controls for the holo projector.

"Yes, but they've all been guarded; locked down tight".

"Not where they needed to be," Zim answered. "You see, almost all of this infrastructure has been in place for decades,"

"Some of it for over a hundred years," Michaels chimed in.

"To prove our theory, we send recovery drones into the Dark Zones in every city where the *Porcelain Death* has been reported since we left New Orleans. What we found was," Zim paused, bringing up a hand full of schematics above my desk, "that each of these systems had major piping running through their Dark Zones. And, when we sent in the little drones to investigate for us…"

Michaels piped up a video from the drone that was sent to Tupelo, Mississippi. In the grainy, greenish night-vision footage, you could see people, using headlamps and old equipment, digging into the forgotten pavement and into the water mains.

"We couldn't catch 'em in the act though; the eventually saw the drone and took the little fella out. But, his last cam footage shows *this*".

Zimmerman brought up a schematic of a miniature pump, complete with a valve the size of my head. "From what we can see here, this is the unit they've putting in place. Otherwise, the system would just show a broken main, and it would be bypassed".

"This way, we can't really tell which line to cut off". I took down the holographic image and turned it around to see more. "It's damned ingenious," I added, hoping in the back of my mind that Charles had not been forced to work on the delivery system as well.

I dropped the image, and sat back in my chair, turning the situation over in my mind. "My guess is that you've already told Forrest, and he's mobilizing everyone he can, and then some?"

"Exactly" Michaels trumpeted, smiling broadly. "Plus, the CDC finished reproducing Charles' formula for the cure en masse; we're sending teams of doctors and nursing staff to all the affected areas to treat folks exhibiting early symptoms".

"We can't save them all Ellie," Zim continued. "But, we can put a stop to this and save as many as we can".

The news was all good; too good, as they say. Something about it just wasn't sitting right in the back on my head.

"Zim, what's the furthest spread point we've gotten so far?"

"Fayetteville, Arkansas," Zimmerman answered, checking his handheld. "No, wait. Now, there's reports' coming in from Branson, Missouri".

"That's far, but… what about Florida?"

Zim plugged away on his handheld again. "Two days ago, there were three cases in Pensacola. All fatal. There's new reports coming in today, but we should get them the cure in time".

Still didn't feel right.

"Anything in South Florida?"

"Wow! Sixteen fatalities in Tampa Bay… five more in Orlando, and… thirty-six in Miami".

Michaels grabbed his comm and started mapping all the cases again. "Redistributing teams to southern Florida, Ellie. Plus, the CDC is sharing the info on how to create the cure, so we should have local facilities turning this stuff out by the gallon by tomorrow morning".

"Boys, they've gone to the left of us, to the right of us, and north of us," I said, finally realizing what was wrong. "So, why aren't there any cases in Mobile yet?"

Zim lost all the colour in his cheeks. Michaels' eyes widened.

"We're too close to New Orleans to not be a target, and we're a larger city that Fayetteville. And I can guaran-damn-tee you that the plumbing that runs under old Mobile is some of the oldest in the south.

I grabbed my comm and pulled up a recovery drone that was assigned to our Dark Zone, setting it in a circular search pattern, widening each loop. It wasn't long before the sensors on the unit started giving us radiation warnings. The recovery drone rounded another corner, and the streets were littered with porcelain-skinned bodies. It reminded me of the ruins of Pompeii, seeing people frozen in time, forever locked in the agony of their death.

"The Preterist *are* already here, boys. And they've got the old version of the virus".

"The one Charles didn't have a cure for," Michaels remarked quietly.

"I'm not sure what they're planning, but I know what I'm planning".

Zim and Michaels both looked at me, then nodded their heads as I drained the last drop of coffee from my cup. "Suit up, boys, and grab a SWAT team. We're going into the Zone, and we're going to stop these bastards once and for all!"

## 28
### ✎Exposure✎

We had a lot to do, and almost no time to do it in. Whatever the Preterist were planning for Mobile, it was different than the murderous horror they were unleashing in other cities. I sent Michaels to grab whatever radiation exposure meds we could get from the pharmacy downstairs, and asked Zim to coordinate a SWAT team for us to head into the Zone. I grabbed my armor weave and a set of light-screen goggles from my office, and pulled my Pulser off her charging station. I also grabbed a few quick-charge clips, just in case.

I'd promised my boys that I'd meet them at the end of Conception Street, and asked them to have the SWAT team meet us there. I still had a lot of things to get done. First, I had to update my boss on the situation. After a quick conversation with Jim, I called my apartment, expecting to find granddad home, since it was almost five o'clock. When no one answered, I figured that he'd gotten home, and gone to bed, so I decided to leave the old man to his rest.

I decided that I needed to review the drone footage as I strapped on my armourweave. The stuff had been improved recently; it was still black, and held on by Velcro and alligator clips, but it could take a shot from a .44 at three feet and ensure that you only had broken ribs from the impact. Funny thing; this new body armour had been tested against every type of firearm and round short of a missile launcher, but I was more worried about how well it would protect against a needle. While the Preterist may have been using the old version of the Porcelain Death, that didn't mean they hadn't found a way to weaponize the liquid form for close combat. And we had no idea how that would behave in the presence of all the radiation they'd let loose in the Dark Zone.

The drone footage had shown the Preterist had camped out in the old Dunbar Magnet School, and from what we could see, they'd set it up like a fortress with all the stuff they'd found in the Zone. Everything from old cars to piles of furniture had been used to block the entryways. Weird thing was, the drone had spotted at least a few dozen of them, Preterist and Pirates alike, but in the last few hours, there had been no movement.

I met my team at the 'end' of Conception Street, one block past Bienville Square, where we'd discovered the body of Preston Woodridge all those months ago. After the incidents in Miami last year, most of the Zones underneath the new cities had been fenced off, and Mobile was no exception. It wasn't locked off; the people there could still come and go, if they wanted to. Of course, I knew that was far easier for someone like me who lived *outside* of the Zone, to move freely across that shadowy, imaginary border. For those living underneath its wings, moving out, or up, was darn near impossible.

Michaels and Zim stood outside the blockades leading into the Zone, leaning up against a multi-traveler, and chatting with a familiar face.

"Briggs!" I exclaimed, walking up to the SWAT commander from Pensacola, and giving him a quick hug around the neck. "What brings you here?"

"Well, to be honest, Agent Dyett," he started, getting a look from me. Briggs paused, and started again, "To be honest, Ellyandra, my men and I heard that you needed a team for a difficult, dangerous mission. As kind as you've always been to us," he paused looking around to his men, who all nodded in agreement, "we volunteered. If you need help - we'll give it".

The last time we'd worked with Briggs and his men was around two years ago, when we had to clear out evidence from the old County Hospital, and ended up coming face to face with one of the roving gangs in the Zone. And now, here they were, standing ready to die if it would help.

"Briggs," I began; but this time, *he* gave *me* a look. "Liam," I responded, seeing that look turn into a smile, "this one is much more dangerous than last time. There's radiation in the area already, and a few versions of a mutated virus that could,"

"Turn us to stone; yes, ma'am". Briggs grabbed his comm and gently wiggled it in his hands before putting it back. "I read the synopsis, Ellie. So did my team. And," he paused, gesturing around to his men, "here we are, regardless".

One thing Granddad had always taught me was the value of good people. As he used to say, *'don't judge people just on what they do or don't do for you; look at their reasons, look at their drives'*. The men around me had no reason to be here, other than their wish to help make the world a better place. And while, in this case, they *were* helping me, something inside told me that, even if another agent had sent out this call, they would have responded.

I waved my boys, and the SWAT boys, into a huddle. "Ok, just like last time, right?" I asked. "We get in, we do what we need to do! *NO ONE* is left behind! RIGHT?"

"RIGHT!" came back the resounding answer.

"Alright then!" I replied. Load up, and head in".

\*\*\*\*\*\*\*

On a map of Old Mobile, the destination only looked like a few blocks away. In reality, it was slow going. As usual, when we entered the Zone on the multi-traveler, there were people scattering and hiding. They'd come to mistrust everyone, and with good reason. Plus, with all the derelict cars, trucks and vans that were left rotting in the streets, we couldn't just simply drive with ease to our destination. Besides, as sad as it was, people *lived* in these vehicles. We moved gingerly through the first few blocks, until we started finding the stone-skinned bodies that the recovery drone had shown us earlier.

Zim was watching his comm, waiting for a sign that we'd entered a radiation zone. Michaels reached out and handed me three pills the size of my thumb.

"What the hell do I do with these, Aaron? Make myself a burger?"

"These are the radiation exposure meds you asked for" he answered. "Sadly, you are supposed to swallow them whole".

Zim didn't even look up, responding, "Damn near choked to death, so let's hope they are worth it".

I took the first of the pills; it was smaller than the others, but it took half of my water and a lot of willpower to down it. Michaels refilled my canteen, and pointed to the second pill. While it was larger, it had been made more narrow. As much as I *hated* swallowing pills, this one did go down easier.

Then, there was the third pill.

My mom had often told me about childbirth; specifically, *my* birth. How long it took what the level of pain was, etc… When I swallowed that pill, the only thing I could think of was that it was like childbirth in reverse. Here I was forcing something that felt like the size of a watermelon, into an opening the size of my nose (although it was my throat). I gagged a few times, before finally forcing the 'horse-pill' down, and draining my refilled canteen to chase the evil that I'd just put into my body.

"Thanks a lot, Aaron," I said, my voice more raspy than usual.

"No worries, Ellie," he answered, smiling demurely. I reached out and smacked him on the shoulder, just because.

Briggs leaned over in the traveler, getting close to my ear so I could hear. "Ellie, the radiation just kicked in. We're getting close".

I looked over to Zim, who nodded at me. Shaking an affirmative to Briggs, I pulled my pulsers, and gave the order to 'stop us half a block outside the school'. Briggs nodded, and turned back to his driver. We were going much more slowly now, almost at a crawl. The number of porcelain bodies had increased. Every few feet, the traveler's wheels would hit a corpse, shattering it into dust. There was just no way around it; there were too many of them, who'd died anonymously in the forgotten streets, in a most horrible way.

"Stop here," I ordered. The traveler came to an abrupt halt. Once the electronic motor was disengaged, there was a near-perfect silence.

****

We found the Dunbar School exactly where we knew we would, but instead of a firefight, we were met with barricades, traps, and silence. With gentle, well-planned steps, we easily entered the school.

The silence cried out in deafening tones.

We knew they were there, in the shadows, but no matter how much ground we took and claimed for our own, there was no response. And honestly, that made the silence and darkness of the Zone more frightening than ever. We *knew* they were there. We just didn't know where.

They could be anywhere; so they *were* everywhere.

Zim and I signaled to the rest of the group that we were breaking off, and pointed to the old gym to let them know which way we were going. In a situation like this, we had chosen long ago to use radio silence, just in case. Briggs and Michaels gave an acknowledgement, and Zim and I headed toward the gym.

The doors were the old, metal, creaky doors one would expect from a building of this age. And, as we looked over the old maps, we soon found there was no other way in. So, Zim and I took a deep breath, readied our weapons, and barged into the gym.

The groan of the metal doors echoed in the silence, reverberating until the last breath of the closing doors had given its last. On each side of us, there were raised bleachers built into additional levels of the room. They had fallen silent, with no shadows dancing about to give away any sentient presence. The same could be said of the stage that ruled the far wall; its curtains had been called long ago, and sat on the sides of the stage in dirty, rotten tatters. But the stage itself lay as silent as the darkness around us.

It was the center of the room that was casting shadows, but none of the dark figures created by the firelight responded to our presence. Standing around the campfire that burned in the center of the room were at least a dozen, motionless figures.

Initially, Zim and I both took defensive positions, but we soon realized that there was no response from our obvious entrance. We carefully crept towards the fire, and the people who surrounded it, keeping Pulsers focused as we moved. But, after we crossed the fifty-ish feet of distance, still with no response, we lowered our weapons and approached the figures.

They were all dressed in the Preterist garb, and they were all as solid a stone as I'd ever seen, their skin gleaming in the firelight as would any well-polished, porcelain plate or picture.

The Preterist had fallen victim to their own image of Death. And *He* had taken them, in his mercy.

## 29
### ❧Entrapment❧

I looked around the silent camp, studying the faces of the men and women who stood lifeless around the dancing campfire. Here, there was no sadness, no fear, no struggling against impending death; there was only the simple, healthy look of happy people, frozen in a moment forever. While the non-radioactive version or the *Porcelain Death* killed without the cure in a given timeframe, the stronger, more potent version killed almost instantly, as the virus was inhaled or absorbed, and multiplied exponentially in milliseconds. Looking at the smiling faces of the statues around the campfire, in the middle of the gym, I saw no fear, no pain... only the happiness that comes from giving oneself over to the will of another, without a thought or a care. It's the same look that a toddler has while playing in the mud, the same obvious joy that a forever child has getting into the refrigerator and playing with all the food. It was the joy of being free from responsibility; the joy of an infant who hasn't realized that *they* cause anything to happen in the world around them.

It was the joy of ignorance, and as much as I hated what they'd been a part of, as I looked on their chiseled faces, I could only feel pity for them.

We stood in the camp the Preterist had made, looking at their departed faces, captured in stone-like precision for the ages. Zimmerman was checking for radiation signatures, and he found them scattered all over.

"El, I'm getting hits on rads here, here and…" he stopped as he scanned each of the dead Preterist, "especially here".

I walked over to the space Zim had pointed out, and almost slipped on the floor.

"It's wet. Why would the floor be wet?"

Zim stepped cautiously over to me, scanning the water with his handheld. "It's water Ellie. It' HEAVY water; like, from an old nuclear reactor".

"Like Fukushima". Zim nodded. "Guess that answers the question of what was actually *in* the metal vial".

Sure enough, a quick search of the area turned up another one of the vials, with the same markings as the one we'd recovered from the crashed plane.

"Make sense, Ellie. You can't bottle radiation".

"But you can bottle something that is radioactive" I said finishing his thought. I tossed the vial aside and looked back to the Preterist, stuck in silence around the fire.

"We can't help these folks, Zim," I said, re-examining their glazed-over faces in the flickering light. "But, something isn't right".

"What's that El?" Zim asked, uploading his info to the group datalink.

"Where are the pirates?"

Zim stopped, and looked around at the corpses that surrounded us. None of them were in the uniforms of the pirates that we'd seen on the drone's video feed.

Zim looked at me, cautiously moving his hand towards his pulser. "El, I think we may have found a problem".

Suddenly, a bullet crossed right in front of me, shattering the body of the Preterist nearest me. I only had time to shout out 'COVER!" before more gunfire rang out, each volley causing a reverberation in the echoing space we were in. Zim made it to some nearby boxes, and I hid behind the dead Preterist. One of the bullets struck a nearby corpse, who shattered into pieces like a ceramic vase.

"I think we found the Pirates, Ellie!" Zim called out. I reminded myself to slug him for that one later.

"Call in our backup!" I commanded, adding, "then give me cover!" Zim acknowledged by hitting a few controls on his handheld, then stood from his hiding place, and leveled several shots from his Pulser in the general direction of the gunfire. He must've hit a few of them at least, because the rounds that were coming towards us diminished.

From the back of the gym, on either side of the stage, there were exits that led not only backstage, but into the rest of the school. I'd imagined there were also stairs that led up to the bleachers, so I took off for the backstage area, in hopes of finding a non-direct way to reach the men who were firing on us.

The SWAT team, with Briggs and Michaels at the front, came bursting through the doorway of the gym, splitting up to hit the far stairs that led to the bleachers. I kept to my course, heading backstage, and around the corner of the cinderblock walls, looking for another way up.

Just as I rounded the corner, I saw Tiermo, standing with two of his men. When they saw me, Tiermo smiled the biggest, creepiest smile I'd ever seen, and stepped away, walking briskly down the hallway behind him. His men drew their weapons, but I'd already had my pulser out and ready. I dropped them both easily with one shot, and ran down the hallway to catch Tiermo.

Taking just a brief second, I grabbed my comm and said, "Zim, Michaels, Briggs. Tiermo is here; backstage. I'm going after him!" Not waiting for a response, I shoved my comm back into its pocket in my armourweave, and placed my body flat against the wall of the hallway, gingerly stepping along to follow Tiermo.

There were more twist and turns than I could really keep up with. I was so focused on chasing down the man who'd injured my family, hunted me... who'd killed a friend that I loved, it didn't surprise me that I was almost too single minded. A few more turns here and there, and I made it to another building altogether. It was a creaking metal door that echoed its movement down the abandoned, buried body of the old school, that set me in the right direction. I found my way to the Cafeteria, and took a moment to look through the dirty, single pane of glass that that was inset in the door. In the next room, there was another fire, and sitting next to the fire, was a figure. Through the small, filthy window I couldn't make out the details, so I took a deep breath, raised my pulser close to my head, and threw the door open, taking immediate aim at the seated figure.

I almost threw up when I realized that it was my grandfather. He sat, unbound in the chair, fedora slightly cocked to one side. When he raised his face to look at me, I could see patches of glossy, porcelain-looking spots were already forming on his cheeks, and had glazed over one eye completely.

"Granddaddy!" I said, in shock and disbelief.

"Ellie," he started, barely able to speak, "Behind ..."

Not only had I been led into a trap, but the bait was assured to keep me there. Out of the darkness, Tiermo had crept up behind me, and smashed the butt of his firearm against the back of my skull.

There wasn't time to respond. My eyes lost focus, and I passed out before I could take any steps to defend myself. Tiermo had me, and my grandfather. In the dark, decaying buildings of the Zone, we lay wounded, and one of us was already dying from a virus that should never have existed.

# 30
## ⮜Death⮞

Honestly, if someone was going to knock me out, I'd prefer a shot with a fully charged taser than being clubbed into unconsciousness. While the headache I woke with was about the same, the dizziness and blurred vision were actually worse.

I woke to find myself sitting in another chair, about twenty feet away from my grandfather. Between us, Tiermo stood with his back to the old man, facing me. He'd placed a small table between us. A quick attempt to move told me that I was tied up. So, just like I had in Miami, I pulled a little hook inside my sleeve that released the rope eating nanites that had saved me before. I could only hope now that they would work as well as they did last time.

Tiermo was the first to speak. "Well, well, well," he began. "So here we are again. You just keep coming up in my life, and I don't like that". Tiermo turned to look at my grandfather, whose breathing had become more shallow. "But I don't think you'll run away, will you?"

"How dare you bring him into this, Tiermo". The obvious scowl on my face was so sour it almost hurt, but the utter hatred I felt for Tiermo had finally come to a boil, and there was no holding it back. I wiggled my hands slightly, and felt a tiny bit of give in the ropes I was bound with.

"You signed all your deaths when you destroyed what I had built in Miami!" Tiermo stood from behind the small table, and began pacing menacingly. "Drove me off to live as a damn pirate. I went from being a king to almost starving to death". Walking over to me, he bent down and almost whispered into my ear, "Tell me, Ellyandra; do you believe in Divine Intervention?"

He stood up again, and walked behind the table, never taking his eyes off mine. "Well, *do you*?"

I refused to answer. Tiermo sat back down on the other side of the table. "Heh heh, you see, I didn't. All I had was my hatred of you. But then, we were hired by Jeremiah Power, and *all that changed*".

"Everything I needed for my revenge was handed to me on a Golden Platter, and *you* helped do it".

"How so?" I asked, not raising my voice. The ropes were giving just a little bit more. I just needed to buy some time.

"When you brought down Waldorf two years ago, you opened up a can of worms". Tiermo sat back in the chair, placing his hands behind his head, and propping up his feet on the cloth-covered table. "Once word got out about his experiments, crackpots from all over the world wanted a piece of that pie. And Jeremiah Power hired us to go get him a slice".

"That entire record was sealed Tiermo," I answered back. "So how would anyone…"

"You think Cano and I were the only 'bad apples' at the FBI?" Tiermo stood again, moving toward me. "Come on, Ellie; even you aren't that naive". He got right by my face again, almost whispering, "Are you?"

"No, I'm not". I nodded over to my grandfather, who looked like he'd passed out in his chair. "But why bring him in on this?"

Tiermo laughed loudly, moving back to the other side of the table. "Why? To HURT YOU, of course!" Once again, he sat. "But, I have my plans, and I'm even going to give you something you never gave to me".

"What's that, Tiermo?" My bonds were almost broken. I only needed a few more minutes.

"A choice". With this, Tiermo pulled away the cloth that had covered the table, revealing on one side, three or four syringes, and on the other, two metal vials of what I now knew was radioactive heavy water, and a small, flat jar full of white powder.

"You can't be serious, Tiermo!"

"Oh, but I am," he calmly responded. "Here is the choice I give you. Pick one of these, and I'll use it to end your life. Refuse, and *I* choose; but," he paused, looking back to my grandfather, "if I have to choose, then once your mother and the girls are found, they will all die, with just as much pain and fear as your beloved grandfather". The smile on his face was maniacal, as he waited for me to fully grasp what he was telling me.

"So I choose to die, and the girls live? How do I know you'll keep that promise?"

"I've made no promise to keep; just... a statement that I won't actively seek them out".

I tested my bonds again, with a little more success. I knew that the injectible form was, if not more painful, at least not as fast. Worst case scenario, that choice still gave me some time.

I nodded to the right side of the table. Tiermo smiled, grabbing a syringe, and approaching me. "I'd hoped you'd go for the one where you think you have hope. It's far more enjoyable to watch you wither away and die slowly!"

Tiermo knew better than to free my arms. He opened the collar of my armourweave, and slowly started caressing my neck and collarbone with the end of the needle.

"What's the matter, Tiermo?" I asked mockingly. "Can't get up the courage to do it?"

"Oh no," he said with a devious smile, "I plan on making this last as long as possible". With that, he pierced the skin near my jugular, just a tiny bit, but pulled out the needle without plunging the virus into my body. He traced the needle slowly along my neck again, and did the same on the other side, leaving the end of the medical device in my flesh just long enough to twist and turn it about, before he pulled it out again.

He unbuttoned my undershirt, and started placing the needle between my breast, making little circular motions up and down between my bosoms.

I was squirming, not only to get away from the needle, but to put pressure on the weakened ropes that were binding my hands. I looked over to my grandfather, who I'd just seen sitting by the fire, but now, the seat was empty.

"You know what?" Tiermo asked, placing the needle over my left breast, and taking aim at my heart. "I think I'd rather watch you suffer while dying!"

The rest is still a blur to me. Tiermo raised the needle, but as he did so, my dying grandfather, who'd taken one of the other syringes off the table, came up behind Tiermo, stabbing him in the neck and plunging the viral-laden liquid into him. Tiermo, in turn, swung his arm around and injected my grandfather, and the two of them began to struggle.

As the men fought, and moved away from me, my bonds were finally free, and I jumped up to grab the only weapon I could see. When Tiermo turned back towards me, having knocked my grandfather out again, he approached only to find me standing. Reaching for his gun, he simply wasn't fast enough; there was no way he could have stopped me from tossing the radioactive water onto his torso. Nor could he respond when I took a handful of the deadly white powder, and blew the lot of it right into his face.

Blinded and coughing, Tiermo dropped his gun, and grabbed at his eyes. Even in the low firelight, I could see the transformation starting to take effect. He made a few halted, menacing steps toward me, then fell to the ground, shattering into rubble.

I didn't waste any time on Tiermo's body. I just ran to my grandfather's side, and lifted him into my arms. Grabbing my comm, I called out for Zim and Michaels, and activated my beacon. They'd find us soon, but I wasn't sure if it was already too late.

"Did ya get him, Ellie?" Granddad asked, barely able to speak.

"Yes Sir!" I answered, tears turning my vision into a total mess.

"Good girl, hon". Granddad raised his hand toward my face, the cold porcelain of his fingers gently caressing my cheek. "Love you Ellie".

"Love you, Granddaddy" I responded, as he passed out.

# 31
### ❧Funeral❧

The cure that Charles McFarlane had created was used on my grandfather, but a lot of damage had already been done. We brought him home, so however many days or weeks he had could be spent, as he said, really living as much as he was capable.

I had been lucky. Even after physically handling the dust of the Porcelain Death, I never contracted the condition. Zim and Michaels believed that the anti-radiation meds I'd taken protected me. I just thought I was lucky.

Federal agents finally cornered Jeremiah Power outside of D.C., and seized all his equipment and his liquid virus samples before he could do any further harm. The rest of the Preterist were rounded up, city by city. Some put up a fight, and died in doing so. Others peacefully surrendered, turning over the whereabouts of other cells in the process.

Forrest ended up taking a few months off, for recovery and, as he said, a *bit of sanity*. What he'd been through had taken its toll, if not physically, mentally. Sandra told me later that it was months before he stopped waking every night, nearly jumping out of bed in a fit of terror. As for me and the rest of my boys, we too took off for a few months. We'd earned it.

My girls and my mother came home. Now that we were all safe, the U.S. Marshal Service brought them out of protective custody. The girls were so happy to see me, but even more happy to see Granddaddy. I think that, if Granddad hadn't come home, they would have always blamed themselves. Even banged up and looking much older than he had before, my girls were in tears as they joyously hugged the old man. Looking into his eyes, I could see that the feeling was mutual. That first night that they were home, they snuck into Granddad's room after he'd fallen asleep, and gently snuggled Chester in next to him, to keep an eye on him.

My family was safe, but the hardest parts were still to come.

********

All in all, over twenty-two thousand people had been infected by the *Porcelain Death,* but thanks to the sacrifice of Charles McFarlane, around eighteen-thousand of them recovered fully. Of course, we'd never really know how many people in the Zones had fallen victim. There were too many undocumented, non people living there. But treating the water supplies around the southeast had surely saved tens of thousands more.

The Government had held onto Charles body during the *Porcelain Death* crisis, so once that had passed, his remains were turned over to Julie McFarlane, his mother, and funeral plans were made. I was shocked when I received a handwritten letter from his mom, asking me to eulogize Charles. Of course, I accepted.

Julie and I hadn't seen each other in years. When we'd last spoken, she was doing what any mother would do; she was taking up for her son, and that conversation hadn't gone well for either of us.

Now, standing outside on the steps of the Cathedral Basilica in Downtown Mobile, the small, older woman looked lost and fearful, peering from behind a black veil, staring out at a world where her pride and joy, where her beloved son, was no longer alive.
When I approached her, Julie simply placed her arms around my shoulders, buried her face beside my neck, and quietly held onto me for a while. Over time, she and I would end up speaking more and more, and it was a relationship that I chose to nourish. Even with all its ups and downs, we had more in common than just the fact that we'd loved Charles McFarlane. But, ask yourself this; sometimes, isn't something like that enough?

Archbishop Hartley led the service, with all the traditional trappings of a Catholic funeral. It was funny to me, since Charles had always been Agnostic. He wasn't Atheist, as you might expect a scientific mind like his to be. His take was that if there was a God, and it couldn't be proven one way or another, that you couldn't discount the possibility. That being said, Charles had never been a religious man, and here we were, honoring his memory in a way that would have made him uncomfortable.

Eventually, it was my turn to speak. On my way to the pulpit, I stopped and leaned down to

Charles' mom, and asked her, "Do you trust me, Julie?" She nodded, and I kissed her on the forehead, then moved to take my place as speaker.

"Charles McFarlane was an unmitigated ass," I began. A small murmur ran through the crowd, but I continued, undaunted. "He was arrogant, rude, and without shame or humility". The crowd again, rustled uncomfortably.

"But, I loved him". I stopped for a moment, feeling more emotional than I'd expected. "For all his failings, for all his arrogance, I loved him".

People were no longer shuffling in their pews uncomfortably, so I continued. "He was a brilliant scientist, who contributed more to the world in his years than most do in a lifetime. He was gifted beyond words. And," I stopped again, realizing that I was crying, "and he saved a lot of lives with one of the most selfless, generous acts that I have ever known anyone to make."

"I could stand here for hours telling you things that you already know about Charles McFarlane, but I won't do that. Instead, I'll ask you, as his friends, colleagues and family, to ask yourselves, if you would have made the same sacrifice to save the people you love; to save people you'd never even meet. And know that, if that time ever comes for you, Charles led by example. For all his faults and failings, for all his brilliance and capability, he made a choice that was not based on science or self-preservation.

"He made a choice based off of what he knew to be right. He made a choice, out of love".

After I finished, the procession took his body from the Sanctuary, and into the waiting hearse. But, I couldn't do the graveside service. It was just too much. Plus, since the man had literally died in my arms, I didn't need the closure. It would be a long time before I ever felt any closure with Charles. And that was OK.

********

In the end, I lost two important men in my life because of the Preterist and their *Porcelain Death*. We had about a month with my grandfather home, but in the end, too much damage had been done, and the stresses of the physical fights, and what his body went through both succumbing to, and fighting off the virus, proved to be too much for the old fella. After one particularly good meal, and a great evening playing with the girls, and talking to me and mom for half the night, Granddad went to bed, and to sleep eternal.

When I found him the next morning, he was laying on his back, with a smile on his face. Chester was tucked under his left arm.

For all the grieving we did, the girls were actually a lot stronger than I'd expected. They were just glad that *'granddaddy wasn't alone - that he'd had Chester with him'.* Mom surprised me too, simply leaning over to her father, kissing him on the forehead, then saying, "Love you too, Daddy".

Mom had set the memorial service for the next weekend. I arrived, dressed in black, with the girls in simple white gowns. Chester had been given a white tie for the event. We got out of Deloris, and headed to the event hall where the ceremony was to be held, and met Michaels, Forrest and Zimmerman at the door.

Hugs were graciously exchanged, and Olivia nearly toppled Forrest trying to jump into his arms. When I opened the door, the faint sounds of music poured out into the evening air. Forrest looked at me and raised an eyebrow, but I just shrugged my shoulders and said, "Mom and Granddad had this all planned a long time ago. I have no idea".

We entered the main room to find it brightly lit, with a live jazz band set off to one side, playing classics. All around, people were talking, dancing, drinking, and most importantly, they were laughing. My mother had set up little video players throughout the room, and on each one, there was a video of Granddad telling jokes, or cutting up with some person or another.

Mom came up to us and hugged us all one by one, keeping the girls close to her as we talked.

"Mom, is *this* what you two had planned?" I asked, confused.

"Yep!" Mom answered with a smile. "Look around you love; no one is sad, no one is crying or broken. The only tears you will see here tonight are tears of laughter and joy and that my love is what Daddy always loved about life".

"This is how he wanted to be remembered," I replied, looking around the room. It was filled with people much older than me, much younger than me, and every age in between. I guess I'd never really realized that Granddaddy didn't just belong to me and my family. A man like that belonged to everyone, and loved everyone as much as he could.

Erin and Olivia ran off to play with some other kids in the back of the room, and after a while, I loosened up a bit. Mom and Aunt Chele ended up both dancing with me at one point, and the food and music didn't trail off 'til well after midnight. In the middle of the room, on a small table, sat an urn, where the ashes of my grandfather rested, watching all the people he loved remember him, and enjoy their lives.

I sat in a recliner, near the end of the night, watching Jim and Michaels carry Erin and Olivia out to my waiting vehicle. Looking around the room, I realized something important.

Two men had shown me so much, shown me a better world. Now, that Mantle passed to me. We still lived in a world where people lived and died daily in the Zones, forgotten and lost in the darkness. We still had corruption, and sadness. We still had evil people. And we always would. But, thinking of the world I wanted to build for my girls, I knew I'd happily take the legacy of both my friend, and my grandfather, and do my part to make the world better.

In the end, what else can you do?

## ❧Epilogue❧

On New Year's Eve, the girls wanted to stay up and watch the ball drop, so I decided to keep myself busy by going through a few items of Granddads. It was around eleven-thirty when mom had to wake the girls so they wouldn't miss the ball drop in New York. She'd decided to move in with us, since Granddad was gone. While she said it was to 'help with the girls', I knew better. Mom was already in her early sixties; losing her father so late in life was a blow that, despite all the love and kindness, had changed her world in ways she didn't want to face alone.

I made sure she wouldn't have to.

I went to granddad's room and pulled out a box from earlier this year, and settled in at the back of the living room, to quietly go through it.

Turns out, I'd pulled the box from granddaddy's trip with the girls to Vermont. While the girls had each kept their cameras (and used them almost daily) granddad had left his packed for some reason. I turned the unit on, and started shuffling through the pictures that were still on the memory card.

On the small screen built into the camera, I saw images of bright blue skies, blinding white snow, and my little girls, with their stuffed rabbit held between them, running about in snow pants, throwing snowballs, and generally having the time of their lives. They kids had told me that, despite the Spring Thaw, Granddad had found a few mountaintops where the snow was still clean and new. I'm not sure what all was going on that day, but after a few dozen pictures, the single images stopped. All that was left on the memory card was a video.

"Mamma! Mamma! It's almost time!" Erin said loudly. Olivia added, "It's almost 2057!"

I looked at mom, and said, "I thought it was almost 23:59". She chuckled as the girls scratched their heads. Military time had always been source material for a good joke (or a bad pun) in our family.

I turned back to the video on Granddads camera, and decided to hit play. On the small screen, the snow-laden field they'd been playing in came into view. The sky was cloudless, and the bluest blue you could imagine, with the sun shining bright, alone and unchallenged in the sky. As the camera panned across the landscape, granddad started talking.

I hadn't expected that. And as much as I had known that I had missed his voice, it was both unsettling, as well as comforting.

Off in the distance of the video, I could see my girls running around. Granddad called out, "Don't go too far away loves; head back over this way!"

He followed them with the camera. In the background of the room, I could hear the New Year's countdown begin. On the smaller screen, I heard my grandfather talking again.

"You may not know it Ellie, but I'm damn proud of you. I look at these girls, the girls you *chose* to love, and I think that it's the best choice you've made in your entire life".

*'...30, 29, 28...'*

Granddad continued talking as the girls ran through the snow towards him. "I don't know what time I have left, my love, but the last few months, with you, your mom, these girls... there's nothing I won't do for you. For any of you."

*'...13, 12, 11...'*

I looked back to the small video, to see my girls crashing into the old man, and the camera being tossed about, mixing snowy hills and sky, and the sound of laughter rising up above all else.

"No matter what happens Ellyandra, never forget just how much your granddad loves you".

The video stopped at this point, with his face frozen on the screen, in the sweetest smile. My mom and the girls were saying *' 3, 2 1.... HAPPY NEW YEAR!'*

I put the camera down, and joined them, snuggling my girls tight. Leave it to my grandfather, even in his absence, to find a way to start the New Year with a fresh perspective, and a loving heart.

finis

www.ingramcontent.com/pod-product-compliance
Lightning Source LLC
Chambersburg PA
CBHW020819180626
46814CB00001B/23